I0847386

LOVE YOU A LATTE

Corina Bair

Cover art by Chelsea Kemp

First edition, June, 2025

ISBN: 979-8-9909467-2-9
ISBN: 979-8-9909467-3-6

To all the girls, gays, and theys.

May you never lose your sparkle.

Hello lovely romance readers,

I have two important things to share with you before you read Love You A Latte.

First, this story takes place in a queer-normative world. There are multiple characters who are part of the LGBTQ+ community, but they do not experience discrimination, prejudice, fear of coming out, or any of the atrocities we experience in the real world by being part of this community. I understand that the characters' experiences are not representative of the world we live in, and I have done this intentionally. I hope you find relief in not only the lack of conflict and hate, but the unconditional love and acceptance this book brings. (And yes, there's still Pride, because this is a work of fiction, so why not?!)

Second, although this is a feel-good contemporary romance novella, please review the content warnings:
- Toxic/emotionally manipulative exes
- Workplace harassment/stalking
- Open door sex scenes

Thank you, and happy reading!
Corina

Addison's TayList (because yes, she's a Swiftie)

You Need To Calm Down
Long Story Short
Dress
Maroon
I Can See You (Taylor's Version)
Mirrorball
Me! (feat. Brendon Urie)
Evermore (feat. Bon Iver)
Sweet Nothing
You Belong With Me (Taylor's Version)
Daylight (Live From Paris)
Sparks Fly (Taylor's Version)
I Can Do It With a Broken Heart
All Of The Girls You Loved Before
A Place In This World
New Romantics (Taylor's Version)
*We Are Never Ever Getting Back Together
(Taylor's Version)*
Cruel Summer
Bejeweled
This is Me Trying
The Very First Night (Taylor's Version)
How You Get the Girl (Taylor's Version)
Everything Has Changed (Taylor's Version)

Paper Rings
Hits Different
Style (Taylor's Version)
Electric Touch (Taylor's Version)
I'm Only Me When I'm With You
Down Bad
The Best Day
Long Live

CHAPTER ONE

Addison

I'm giddy with anticipation, even though this might be the most low-key "vacation" I've ever taken. House-sitting for my sister and her boyfriend while taking care of their dog? So chill, but it's exactly the escape from reality—ie. work, my toxic ex-girlfriend, and my annoying ex-boyfriend—that I need. It could not have come at a better time.

What could be going better though, is this rental car situation.

"What do you mean my reservation wasn't confirmed?" I ask, trying not to let the irritation slip into my voice. "I have it right here."

I flip my phone around and rest my forearm on the cool counter, showing the email confirmation. My toes tap the tiled floor impatiently.

"I'm sorry ma'am, but there must have been some sort of glitch. We don't have a car for you," says the young man behind the computer.

I fist my hand, hidden by the counter, and take a deep breath.

"That's fine, forget the reservation. I'll take whatever you have."

"It's... well, sorry, I mean," he stumbles over his words, looking ready to cry. "We don't have anything left."

"I'm sorry, what?" I ask.

"Well, we're booked, so we don't have any available

cars for you to rent. I'm so sorry."

I glance first to my right, then left, but the lines for the other rental car companies don't look promising.

"Do you have any way of telling who else might have some cars available? Seeing as how I have already paid for one?" I try not to speak through my teeth, I really do, but I don't think I'm successful.

"Let me grab my manager," he says, and ducks away.

Unfortunately, the manager isn't any more helpful, leaving me stuck in the Phoenix airport over an hour away from where I need to be with no car. This is *not* helping my abandonment issues.

I phone my sister, Everly, though I'm not sure what she's going to do since she and Asim left for their trip last night. They're probably laying on a sunny beach sipping mimosas right now.

"Hey Ad, what's up?" Everly says.

"Hey, so I guess my rental reservation didn't go through and they don't have any cars left so I'm kind of stuck at the airport." I'm grumpy, and my brusque tone shows it.

"What? How is that possible?"

"I don't know, but I'm not sure what to do." I sigh as I pull my luggage behind me and trek over to a bench. I switch the phone to my other ear as I sit down and plop my carry-on bag next to me. "I already tried three different rideshare apps and no one's willing to drive all the way out to the middle-of-nowhere Stone Ridge."

"Well, that's annoying," Everly says, and then Asim speaks up.

"You could call Frankie, they'd come get you."

I splutter in protest as my face turns red just hearing their name. "I hardly know Frankie, that's such a long drive, why would they—"

"Oh, good idea! They wouldn't mind, want me to call for you?" Everly asks, oblivious to my inner turmoil.

Do I want to spend over an hour in a car with the person I've been hard crushing on since we flirted during a drinking game, but then rejected my kiss a few months ago? Someone who I have neither seen nor spoken to since? My gut clenches.

No, I absolutely do not.

Unfortunately, I don't seem to have any say in the matter.

"Okay, I just texted them and sent them your number. I'll text you theirs, too, so you can coordinate. If anything else comes up, just let me know!" Everly is far too happy about this situation, but I guess a tropical vacation will do that to a person. "Talk later, bye!"

She hangs up before I manage a desperate, "Wait...".

As I stare at my phone, a little perplexed at the whirlwind change in circumstances, it buzzes with a text.

Unknown number: Hey, it's Frankie.
    Everly said you're in a situation and
    need a ride from the airport?

Me: Hey Frankie, yeah, I'm really sorry
    about this. My reservation got
    messed up and they have no rental
    cars left. If you're able to drive out
    here I'd really appreciate it, but if not
    no worries! I can figure something
    else out [smiley emoji]

Unknown number: No problem. I'll head
    out soon and text you my ETA

I type and then delete a reply, then my fingers jab out a new one. I debate how many exclamation points is too many exclamation points, then realize they're likely seeing the three little dots popping up and down on their end. This is the worst. I finally settle on only one exclamation point, and hit send.

Me: Oh my gosh, thank you so much.
    Okay, sounds good, talk soon!

* * *

I save their number in my phone and shove it in my pocket, then wander back into the terminal in search of food while I wait for Frankie to arrive.

~~~

Unfortunately, despite being hungry a half hour ago, my stomach has been in knots since Everly decided to so very thoughtfully solve my problem for me, so I was only able to manage a few bites while waiting for Frankie. The remnants of my meal end up in the compost bin and I detour through the airport bookstore as I wait, killing time. I somehow manage not to buy anything, a truly impressive feat, and as soon as I receive Frankie's message that they're pulling into the airport, my stomach flips and explodes with butterflies.

Freaking *butterflies*.

I berate myself internally, trying to hammer in the fact that they rejected me only a few months ago, but it doesn't seem to matter. The butterflies are relentless and don't care one bit about how tarnished my heart is.

I mean, it shouldn't have impacted me so strongly. It was one night of drinking games, full of flirting and fun, and I had no reason to take it so personally when they didn't want more at the end of the night. Especially since Frankie is my sister's best friend. Of course they wouldn't want to mess things up with Everly by making out with me. They might even think of me like their own little sister.

The thought makes me cringe, and I shudder to shake it off.

I've always been told I'm overly sensitive. The toxic relationships haven't helped, and add in my parents' deaths when I was only twenty—yeah, it's a recipe for emotional disaster.

So my tender heart was bruised by a rejection from someone I thought felt the same way I did, and apparently it still is even now. Months later.

Frankie rumbles up to the curb in their beat-up old blue pickup truck and I suck in a breath, bracing myself. It's one thing to daydream about them, it's another entirely to see them in person again. I mean, they're just
~~~

so *cool*. With their aviator shades, one hand on the top of the wheel and the other out the open window, black tattoos running up and down both arms. Curly, floppy brown hair on top and shaved on the sides hints at their Mexican heritage, while the Polynesian style tattoo circling their forearm speaks to the other side of their family tree. They adjust their hold on the wheel to park and when they look my way, one side of their mouth quirks up and I blink, realizing I'm just standing here. Staring.

I jolt into action, tugging my heavy suitcase and carry-on with me, when they open the door and step out. Those black combat boots do something to me, causing an enticing, swooping motion in my lower abdomen, but when they reach one hand up to remove their sunglasses and I'm hit with those sparkling hazel eyes... yeah. I'm done for.

One hundred percent a lost cause.

Their crooked grin hasn't abated, and I stumble, tripping over my own two feet when they stick their sunglasses into that perfectly messy hair and rake their gaze up and down my body. That can't possibly mean what my body wants it to. My face turns beet red; I can feel how hot my skin is, and I avert my eyes, looking at the dirty pavement instead of them.

I don't look bad, per se. I'm wearing leggings and an oversized tee, so I don't look fantastic, but it could be worse. I hate that I'm having such a strong reaction to them though, my entire body gravitating toward them and seeking their approval, their interest. I try to remind myself that they don't want me, despite whatever that appreciative look might have implied.

"Hey," I say, clearing my throat as I approach.

Frankie already has the tailgate open, and they reach out to grab my suitcase.

"Hey," they reply, and oh heavens that voice. A perfect alto, a bit husky, and all bad for me.

"Hi," I say, and immediately close my eyes for a moment, trying to hold the regret and embarrassment at bay.

Stupid. So stupid.

Frankie laughs as they latch the tailgate shut and the

truck gives a slight lurch. It's a contagious laugh though, and strangely, it doesn't make me feel like I'm being laughed *at*. Instead, that laugh makes my heart flutter in my chest, a happy little dance at hearing their joy. My smile peeks out as they walk around me to the passenger side, but it drops when they open the truck door for me, standing far too close. Close enough to touch with the smallest movement, if I wanted to. If *they* wanted me to.

When I simply stand there and stare for a moment too long, Frankie clears their throat with a pointedly raised eyebrow and angles their head for me to get in.

This person is dangerous. I don't know if my heart is going to survive the next hour, let alone the next week.

CHAPTER TWO

Frankie

Something's off with Addison. I'm not sure what it is, but the confident, bubbly, sunshine creature I couldn't take my eyes off a few months ago is missing, and in her place is a confused, stammering, lost little puppy.

Still hot as fuck, though.

I shake my head, needing to get my mind out of the gutter. I try not to check her out, but it's nearly impossible. She's my every temptation, and that off-the-shoulder tee showing off a collarbone I want to taste is not making things any easier. I shift on my feet as she shuffles toward me and slides into the passenger seat. It's not my business, but I'm having a hard time not demanding to know what's on her mind, what's happened to her relentless smile.

I round the truck and take us out of the airport, turning on the radio and settling in for the drive back to Stone Ridge. I'm bopping along with my tunes, wind weaving through my hand out the window, when Addison practically yells at me.

"Can we put the windows up?" she shouts to be heard over the music and wind. When I glance over at her, I feel like a jerk.

I was trying so hard to avoid ogling her—to avoid even thinking about her—that I didn't notice how uncomfortable she was. Her beachy hair is a windblown mess and her cheeks are stung red from the breeze, or maybe the heat. I roll up the windows, apologizing as I turn the music down and put on the air conditioning.

The relative silence that descends is awkward, and I struggle to figure out why. How do I bridge this gap between us? Before I can figure it out, Addison starts chattering.

"I can't believe how hot it is, how do you not have the air pumping 24/7?" she says, fanning herself.

I bump the fans up a couple notches.

"I guess you get used to it," I shrug, "sorry for not thinking of that. Feel free to adjust it anytime." I gesture to the dash and she nods.

"Thanks," she says. "And thank you for picking me up. I hope it's not too much of a hassle, I know it's a long drive and especially having to go both directions. I feel so bad for hijacking your day. I'm happy to help out at the coffee shop to pay you back!"

I toss a bemused smile in her direction.

"No worries, it's about time I got out of Stone Ridge anyways," I say.

"What do you mean?"

I glance at her, trying to gauge her reaction. "I've never left. This is the first time."

"Wait, what?" Addison says. "You've never been out of town?"

"Nope."

Addison blinks at me, and I shrug again, turning back to the road.

"I mean... why not?"

"I've just never really cared to. I like our little town, it has everything I need. Nothing has ever given me enough reason to leave."

"Wow, I can't believe you've never left Stone Ridge. Do you want to stop anywhere? I'm not in a rush, I mean besides having to let Moose out, so we can't take too long, but if there's anywhere you want to go," she trails off, glancing at my fingers tapping along to the beat on the steering wheel from the corner of her eye.

I shake my head. "Nah, I'm good, we can just head back."

"Okay. Cool." Addison bobs her head a couple times, and I hold in an amused grin, relaxing back into my seat as I drive.

"So, how's work going?" she asks.

"Yeah it's pretty good, same as usual. Just coffee shop stuff," I reply. "How about you?"

I know she does something in the business world, but I'm not clear on exactly what it is. To be fair though, we didn't do much work talk when she showed up in town a few months ago, the only time I've spoken to her in over eight years. What I don't expect is for her to launch into a full blown rant about the work drama she's currently dealing with. Something about wanting a hybrid position, but her boss being unsure about the feasibility of it. I'm doing my best to follow, but I don't think she's making complete sense. Regardless, my brain jumps into hyper focus when I hear her mention an ex.

"I just don't want to work with my ex anymore. He keeps coming on to me even though we've been split up for years now, and he's been dating someone else. I don't get why he won't leave me alone. I mean I've tried to set boundaries, and I've talked to HR, but they don't seem to care. Everyone thinks he's such a *nice guy* who just wants to help and it makes me seem like a dramatic brat not wanting him around me."

It takes all of my willpower not to interrupt and ask for this asshole's name, but what am I going to do? Jump on a plane and go beat him up? No.

Maybe.

"So anyway, I put in an internal transfer request, but haven't heard back yet. I just really want to get out of there, you know?"

Her big blue eyes turn on me and I've never been more tempted in my life to pull the emergency break. I want to kiss that forlorn look right off her face, then pummel her ex in the throat, then whisk her away to my loft and keep her there forever.

That's completely unhinged.

I force myself to look back at the road. I clear my throat and widen my eyes at myself, trying to get a grip.

"Yeah, that sounds crazy. I'm really glad you're getting out of that situation. When are you supposed to hear back about the transfer?"

If it's not in the next two hours, I fear my spleen might

rupture from how badly I want this for her.

"I was supposed to hear back today, but," she pauses to check her phone, "nope, nothing yet."

Addison sighs as her hands fall to her lap, dejected. My heart falls right along with them.

"What do you like to listen to?" I ask, willing to listen to anything that will bring her smile back, and before I know it, I have her singing along to Chappell Roan with me as we fly down the desert highway toward home.

~~~

"Thanks again for the ride. I really don't know what else I would have done," Addison says.

Her eyes are an impossible shade of blue. Wide and round as she gazes at me from the passenger seat, bright as the sky on the outside with a ring of lighter, pale blue around the center.

"Okay, um," Addison shuffles in her seat as she breaks eye contact and opens her door.

"Right, yeah, no problem," I say, shaking myself out of whatever trance that was as I unbuckle and step out of the truck. I think she might have been casting a spell on me.

I open the back and reach out to grab her suitcase when my hand closes over hers on top of the handle. I look up right as she turns in my direction, and I instinctively squeeze her hand in mine. She's a few inches taller than me, so when her throat bobs with a hard swallow, it's impossible to miss.

"Frankie?" Addison whispers, and I want to hear all the different ways she might say my name.

"Yeah," I say, my own voice quiet and laced with want.

"Um," Addison looks down at our hands on her suitcase, and I jolt, then decide to make the best of it.

I stroke my thumb along the soft skin on the back of her hand, then slip my fingers around and under hers. Addison's eyes shoot back to mine, wider than they were before. I lean forward, and her body mirrors mine until my mouth is just below her ear.

"Let go, sweets," I keep my voice low and soft, eager to see how she'll react.

Her hand springs open, letting go of the suitcase, and I
~~~

shift my grip to her wrist before she can pull away. Her eyes dart between mine, the moment stretching as she wonders what I'll do.

I quirk my lips into a half smile as I squeeze once, then loosen my grip, allowing her to slowly pull away. Addison's cheeks flush and she pulls her hand into her chest, then tucks an errant strand of wavy hair behind her ear. I whistle the last song we were listening to as I pull her bags out and pile them up on the porch for her, right in front of the door. Addison stares at me the whole time until I shut the tailgate and lean against it, crossing my arms.

"I let Moose out and fed him this morning, the key is in the lockbox, you have the code?" I say.

She blinks a few times before registering what I've said and I bite my lip to keep from chuckling.

"Yep, got it right here." She waves her phone as I nod.

"Alright then, let me know if you need anything else. You know where to find me."

"Right! Thanks again," Addison says.

I get back in the truck with a wave, and she returns it a little too enthusiastically, throwing on the fakest smile I've ever seen as I pull out of the driveway.

It makes me angry for some reason, thinking about her soft lips stretched around a fake smile, and I clench the steering wheel as I navigate into town. Addison shouldn't have to fake anything around me. I want the real version of her, not the one she gives to people she doesn't know. My thoughts stumble when I realize that I am one of those people, though. We don't really know each other. We haven't for nearly a decade, despite her being my best friend's little sister. Still, I never want to see that smile again.

I'm planning how to remedy this problem when I unlock the coffee shop's back door to find another unaddressed envelope has been slipped under it. My head jerks up as I whip around, my gaze darting up and down the alley as I walk around the building to check the main street of our quaint little town, but there's no one suspicious to be seen.

My lips pinch with irritation as I step inside and quickly shut the door behind me, locking it while I stoop to snatch up the envelope. I already know what I'll find inside. I have a whole stash of them locked in my desk upstairs. I know I shouldn't open it, that I should probably take it to the police, but I also know there's nothing they can or will do, since it's only a letter.

Against my better judgement, I slip my finger under the corner and rip it open.

I unfold a piece of white printer paper, the words typed in a plain black font:

> No one wants you here. You're just a dumb bitch with no future. I'm going to tell the world what a stupid bitch you are. I'm going to scratch your ugly eyes out. Your little "business" is a failure and a stain on our town. You'll get what's coming to you. And it'll hurt. Wait and see. I dare you.

My jaw clenches in frustration. I have a healthy suspicion that I know who has been sending these letters, but I can't be sure. They all arrive at different times and days, with no name or return address, and they're never postmarked, just slipped under the back door off the alley so I can't even check the street cameras. I want to crumple it in my fist, but instead I shove it back in the envelope and write the date on the outside, then stomp upstairs to my apartment loft and stick it in the desk drawer with the others.

With nothing left to do but prepare for tomorrow, I plod back downstairs to the coffee shop. I take my anger out on the tables and counters as I scrub them down, turning my hand in hard circles against the wood and hoping the satisfaction of a clean space will settle my emotions.

Before I get very far, my frustrated thoughts screech to a stop when I glance out the window and catch a glimpse of light brown, sun-kissed hair. My head jerks up and I straighten with a smile starting to curve my lips, but when I turn to look, it's a stranger. My heart sinks with disappointment as she flounces down the street with an ice cream cone, laughing as she runs across the road to her friends.

I pinch my lips and return to my task, ignoring the fact

that I'm already desperate to see Addison again.

CHAPTER THREE

Addison

I've tried on three different outfits already and I don't feel confident in any of them. Which is frustrating, because I packed all of my favorite, most confidence-inspiring outfits for this trip.

With a huff, I toss on a pair of frayed jean shorts and another slouchy tee, this one white with "here for the girls, gays, and theys" printed on the front. I twist it up on one side and tuck it into my shorts, then thread a hot pink belt through the loops. Flip flops and a floppy sunhat with my heart-shaped sunglasses complete the look.

If I can't achieve confident, then I might as well be comfortable.

Moose, my sister's black lab mix, is already dancing around my legs, eager to go out after being cooped up all day yesterday.

"What do you think, my sweet Moosie Goosie?" I ask him.

His ears perk and his tail whacks my shins.

"Ow, you gotta watch it with that thing."

He doesn't, and his tail proceeds to thwack the door as I snap on a leash. I figure that's got to hurt, but he doesn't seem phased, so what do I know?

"Alright. Walk and then work, yeah?"

His tongue flops out as he pants up at me, which I take for agreement, and we set out for a stroll. I take him on a roundabout path along the river and then into downtown

Stone Ridge. There's only one main road and a couple side streets, with many of the same shops that were here when I was growing up. I didn't get a chance to do much in town when I was here a few months ago, so it's nice to take my time now. A bittersweet heaviness sinks into my chest at seeing how little has changed as I take my time wandering up and down the paths I used to know by heart. It makes me wonder when this stopped being home, and if it ever could be again.

Everyone seems to know Moose, and he seems to know all the people who stop to give him pets and treats, plus where all the water bowls are. Before I know it, he's pulling me through a propped open door and then we're standing inside Roasted Coffee House. I blink and take off my sunglasses, but Moose is still yanking on his leash.

When I look up to see where he's trying to go, I come face to face with Frankie. All glorious messy curls and tattooed forearms, wearing an apron as they drop muffins into a pastry box. They glance up and their crooked smile punches me right in the chest.

I can't help but grin in response, but my joy feels too big, out of proportion, so I bite my lip in an attempt to contain it. They give me a chin nod while angling their head at the empty table near the counter with a quirked eyebrow. Moose is already tugging me that direction, clearly knowing where he's going, so I figure it must be okay to have him in here.

The customer leaves, and Frankie snags a towel to wipe down the counter. Then they throw it over their shoulder as they saunter toward me, black combat boots scuffing the wooden floor.

"Hey Addison," they say.

My tongue feels thick in my mouth. This has never happened to me before. I have great social skills, I can talk to anyone about anything. I'm bubbly and cheerful and fun, everyone says so! So why can't I talk to this one person?

They drag their teeth over their bottom lip and I'm pretty sure they're trying not to laugh. My cheeks heat and I cover them with my palms.

"You good?" Frankie says.

I clear my throat, then nod, but I still can't speak..

"Right, okay. So I'm gonna snag some more to-go cups to restock behind the counter, then I'll be back and we can try again. Yeah?" they say, and I nod again, perhaps a bit frantic this time.

"Cool," Frankie says, spinning on their heel and striding to the back room.

I drop my hands from my face as soon as they disappear from view, then knock my forehead down on the edge of the table. I literally didn't say one word so Frankie had an entire one-sided conversation. Moose looks up at me with concern in his big brown eyes.

"I know. I'm an idiot," I whisper to him.

His tail wags.

I take it as encouragement rather than agreement this time.

When I hear the back door open, I suck in a breath and sit up, refusing to rub my forehead or otherwise look like a fool in front of Frankie again. They're not looking in my direction, though. Their arms are full, muscles flexed under rolled t-shirt sleeves as they carry two boxes behind the counter and drop them to the floor, then nudge them aside so they have room to help the waiting customer.

I try to think of a plan to get over this weird crush. But maybe I don't need to get over it. I'm pretty sure they were flirting with me again, which doesn't make sense after they rejected me a few months ago. Maybe they're a super flirty person and they flirt with everyone.

I decide that must be it, which makes me feel much better, actually. It's not anything to do with me, which means this can be a normal situation. Normal I can do. Normal, I'm great at.

Frankie glances my direction and seems to realize I'm over my weird moment. With a quick grin, they step over and slide into the chair next to me, angling it so they're facing the entrance and can also see the counter.

I decide to speak first this time.

"I'd like to pay you back for yesterday," I say.

Frankie's hazel eyes sparkle. "Yeah? For what?"

"The ride," I say, twisting my hands together in my lap. "I really appreciate it and you saved me a ton of time and money. The least I can do is pay you back."

"Pfft," Frankie waves me off with a huff. "I don't need

or want your money, sweets."

"Okay well, can I help out here or something then? I'd feel better if I could make it up to you somehow."

I think I might be pouting, and based on the fact that Frankie's eyes are focused on my mouth, it might be working.

"And how do you propose making it up to me?" they say, gaze slowly wandering back up to meet mine.

The first thing that pops into my head is definitely not appropriate, and my cheeks heat again at the thought. Their eyes flare the tiniest bit when they dart to my reddened cheeks. So much for being normal, for being in control this time.

"I could..." I trail off, eyes flitting around for any idea that doesn't involve shedding our clothes. "I could help out around here?"

"You know how to make lattes?"

'Well, no."

"Can you bake?"

"Um, I mean," I trail off again with a heavy exhale as I slouch in my seat. No, I don't know how to do anything that might be considered helpful at a coffee shop. Frankie notices my deflation and their eyes widen again. They sit forward and reach one hand toward me, but drop it with a frown when they notice the movement.

"I guess you could always help clean up," they say, then their face transforms with a smirk. "I assume you do know how to use a washrag, at least?"

"Uh," I huff. "Obviously."

Of course I know how to clean, I'm a grown adult. Just because I used to be a spoiled brat doesn't mean I still am. I grumble under my breath.

Frankie laughs, loud and unrestrained, the same as I remember it.

"Did you just growl? That's cute," they say, still chuckling, and I flush again, but their laugh and smile are contagious. I grin back, then reach out a hand to playfully smack their arm.

They track the movement with their eyes, which are bright when they meet my gaze again.

"You just might pay for that someday," they say, and my lower stomach clenches at the husky note in their voice.

"Extra hours?" I quip, and they chuckle again.

"Extra something."

Frankie chews the corner of their mouth, then lightly slaps their hand on the table.

"Well, I gotta get back to it. You working while you're in town?"

"Yeah," I shrug. "I couldn't afford to take the whole week off, so I'm still on the clock a few hours each day. I should probably get back so I can log on."

Frankie nods.

"If you want to get out of the house, you're always welcome to work here."

I glance up from where I was untangling Moose from his leash.

"Yeah?" I ask.

"Yeah, sweets. No point in spending the next week alone if you don't have to," Frankie says, whistling as they turn and saunter back behind the counter.

I duck my head to hide my answering grin, unsure where this bashful side of me is coming from. I haven't felt this way since... well, maybe middle school. I can't remember, to be honest. And being given a nickname, especially from someone I like and admire, feels good. It makes me feel accepted, like I belong here.

~~~

When I get back to Everly's place and Moose has settled down, I kick back on the couch with my laptop. It's hard to turn my thoughts to work after the conundrum that is Frankie, but as usual, my email has several new notifications.

I click through them, deleting, replying, and sorting as needed, until I come to one from Benji. My lips pinch and my heart stalls in my chest.

I've told him over and over not to send me private emails, and I always copy both his manager and mine on any replies I have to send to him. He doesn't seem to care though, continuing to email me for the smallest, most asinine reasons.

Benji and I dated a few years ago, and at first after we
~~~

broke up everything was fine, even though we work together. It was mutual, and we agreed to stay professional, not to let it impact our interactions or quality of work. When I started dating Sabrina a few months later though, he began to change his tune.

He was still polite enough, but everything he said or did had an undercurrent to it. A pinch of passive aggression here, a sarcastic or snide comment there. Always laughed off, and never enough to bring to HR.

I dated Sabrina for about two years, only breaking it off last December when I caught her cheating on me—with Benji. I don't know for sure how long that had been going on, but I suspect about six months, as that's when his behavior got drastically worse. He started making inappropriate jokes and suggestive comments about threesomes with me and Sabrina, then would tell me to "loosen up" or "take it easy" when I got upset. He always believed I was overly sensitive and loved to tell me so.

I know now that my relationship with him was never healthy, but at the time I was young and inexperienced. He was easy to date since we worked together and had the same schedule. I think it was when Sabrina started seeing him on the side that things got bad. I wasn't able to put it together until after the fact, though.

A few weeks after I broke up with her, she showed up on my doorstep. Tearful and full of regret, she asked if we could try again. I almost said yes. I was two seconds from giving in, when she said his name.

She said, "I miss you, and Benji does too."

Apparently, they *both* wanted me back. She'd already tried this tactic when I caught her cheating: saying we could be a trio, that all three of us together would make the perfect "throuple," even going to far as asking me to "just give a threesome a try." I don't have anything against poly relationships, but what I am against is cheating, manipulation, and toxic communication. All of which they excel at.

I said no—again—but apparently neither of them understand that word. Six months later, Sabrina still texts me multiple times a week. Sometimes just to tell me what she's up to, but other times to ask if I've reconsidered. She pleads with me to take her back, to take them both back, telling me that the three of us together would be a dream come true.

Then I have Benji at work sending me completely unnecessary emails every day, I'm pretty sure just to have any excuse to reach out to me. He texts sometimes too, though thankfully not as often as Sabrina. His are so over the top now it would be almost comical if I wasn't being harassed. Telling me I'm "the one" and that he doesn't want to move forward without me being part of their relationship. I've never shown any interest in ethical non-monogamy, being part of a poly relationship, or even a threesome, so I truly have no idea where they got the idea that I'd be interested, but it seems neither of them can let it go.

I used to answer them, but I don't anymore. Now I ignore the messages when I can, and if it's something I need to address for work, I ensure others are on the email chain. It's been months of the same, and instead of giving up, they keep getting more persistent.

So when I see another email from him, not even one day into my vacation, I nearly snap. I let out an unintelligible yell of frustration, startling poor Moose out of a dream. I huff with annoyance at myself, then decide puppy pets are exactly what I need.

I delete the pointless email, set my laptop aside, then slide down to the floor next to Moose.

"Sorry, sweet boy," I whisper, petting his soft ears. His tail thumps the floor and he closes his eyes again, so I pet along his side and scratch his belly, letting the comfort of an innocent soul soothe me.

CHAPTER FOUR

Frankie

I've been in the coffee shop for hours already, but it's barely nine in the morning. I woke up early with startling blue eyes fading from my vision as I blinked into reality, then realized who I was dreaming of and rolled over with a groan. I don't know how Everly would feel about me dating her sister, though I don't think she'd be opposed.

She'd probably love it, so long as I promised to still spend quality time with her too. Regardless of how my best friend may or may not feel about a relationship that may or may not happen, I wasn't going to be falling back asleep. So I rolled out of bed and decided to get a head start on the morning.

While I bake some of the pastries myself, most are from the local bakery down the road. I do easy stuff that doesn't take too much time or effort: banana bread, quiche, the occasional blueberry muffin. Alex, the baker, makes whatever he feels like for me and it always sells. Cookies, pastries, muffins, desserts, even donuts sometimes. He's talented and prompt with his deliveries, overall an excellent business owner to partner with.

Today he dropped off an armload of macarons in a rainbow of colors along with cream cheese muffins and lavender lemon scones.

I tried one of each. They're all delicious.

I think I'm stress eating. Or maybe excitement eating.

The front window keeps pulling my attention, and

every time the door opens I hope it'll be Addison walking in. It hasn't been yet, and I know it likely won't be for some time. I remember when Everly tried to talk to her at nine a.m. when she was visiting last December. She told me Addison wasn't even out of bed yet, and cranky as hell to boot.

I expect the soonest I'll see her is late morning, if at all.

The brunch crowd distracts me for a bit, but time crawls by. Derek, the owner of the only grocery store in town, stalks past across the street, stopping to mean-mug the coffee shop for a solid minute before continuing on his way. He's wanted to know where I source my specialty coffee beans for years; at this point I'm simply refusing to tell him out of spite.

If he was a nice guy I might consider it, but he's not, so I won't. He can continue to try to upsell me with his crappy coffee beans and good luck to him. Jaime, one of the two teenagers I hired a few months ago when Derek threatened to report me for closing during operating business hours, snags my attention, needing help with the cash register. It's another distraction, one more thing to help this morning slog by.

My frown quickly disappears when a familiar dog on a familiar leash pokes his giant wet nose into the glass door.

Addison is here, and if the pastel yellow leather bag is anything to go by, she brought her laptop with her, as I hoped she would. She takes off her bright pink shades as she steps in and offers me a tentative smile. It's better than the fake one from the other day, so I meet it with a grin of my own.

Then, I realize with horror, I don't know what her coffee order is, and that feels like a crime. She tugs Moose up to the counter with her and I nudge Jaime out of the way.

"What can I get you, sweets?" I ask.

Her cheeks tint a lovely shade of pink.

"I'll take an iced latte, please," she says, and I quirk an eyebrow. There's no way that's her full order. She pinches her lips between her teeth as her eyes skim the menu on the wall behind me, then turn to the pastry box. I decide to help her out.

"What kind of milk?"

"Oh, um, oat would be great, if you have it."

"Sure, any flavored syrup?" I hold in my smirk. I knew she wanted more.

"Maybe," she draws out the word as though she really can't decide, and that intrigues me. Perhaps she doesn't have one go-to order.

"Can't decide?" I ask.

"I like cinnamon, but that doesn't feel right today. Maybe hazelnut? Or vanilla," she trails off, scanning the line of syrup bottles behind me.

"You open to a surprise?" I ask.

Her baby blues snag my gaze as they swing back to me, lighting up with excitement.

"Sure! I love surprises. Just not peppermint," she says.

"In the middle of summer?" I scoff. "I'm not a heathen, Addison."

She grins and requests a rainbow of macarons to go with her latte. I tell her I'll bring everything to her when it's ready and she heads over to a table to set up. Jaime snags a water bowl for Moose while I whip up an iced coconut latte for her.

When I carry over a colorful plate of macarons and her coffee, I notice she's frowning at her phone. Her eyebrows are pinched and she's bouncing her leg under the table.

"Hey," I say, setting everything down next to her. "Everything okay?"

"Oh, yeah!" she says, flipping her phone down on the table and directing another fake smile my way.

"Don't do that," I scold, my voice coming out more harsh than I intended.

Her smile falls and a look of confusion takes over her pretty face.

"Don't do what?"

"Pretend. Don't pretend with me," I say, softening my voice. "I can tell something's bothering you, and if you don't want to talk about it that's okay, but don't with that fake smile."

She breaks eye contact and looks down at the back of her phone, tracing the marbled pattern with the tip of her finger.

"Your real one is far too pretty, and I'd rather know the real you than a fake version, smiling or not," I say, sitting down next to her. Jaime can cover the counter for a bit.

Addison is quiet, but I let her have a moment, realizing I came on pretty strong.

"I don't know what to say to that," she finally says, peeking up at me through a fringe of long, dark lashes.

"That's okay. Do you want to talk about what that frown was for?"

She shakes her head, and I nod my acquiescence.

"What's on the docket for today, then?" I ask.

"Eh, just typical work stuff. Emails, responding to requests, that sort of thing."

"I take it you haven't heard back about the transfer yet?" I say.

She looks up at me with her eyebrows raised. "No," she says slowly, "I haven't. I'm surprised you remembered."

I quirk my lips to the side. What she doesn't realize is that it's not hard to remember everything she says. In fact, to forget anything about this stunning creature would be impossible.

"I remember everything about you," I say, though it's so low under my breath that I'm not sure she hears. I don't think I want her to, not yet anyway.

Whether she does or not, she doesn't answer. I stand so we can both get back to work.

"You staying for a while?" I say.

"I was thinking I would, if that's okay," Addison says.

"I'd love that. Maybe later we can take a break for lunch?"

"Sure," she says, another small smile lighting her face.

~~~

I can't keep my eyes off her over the next couple of hours. Her fingers fly across her keyboard, her perfectly shaped eyebrows pinch and relax, and every few minutes she reaches down to scratch Moose behind the ears. When she finishes her latte, I make her another, this time with caramel instead of coconut. I drop it off without a word, swiping her empty plate and cup, and she gifts me with a slightly bigger smile this time. I wink at Addison as I pass, heading to the next table.

As soon as she sits back and shuts her laptop, I'm
~~~

practically flying across the room.

"Hungry for some lunch?" I say, but she shakes her head.

"You can eat though, I'm happy to still hang out with you for a bit."

I shrug and lean back in the chair, widening my legs and kicking my feet out so one bumps into hers. She glances down as though she can see through the table, then back up, her eyes scanning my face. I tilt my head with another smile, waiting for her to say whatever is on her mind.

"Why didn't you kiss me?" she blurts, then slaps her hands over her mouth as her eyes flare with panic.

I freeze, sensing the hush that's fallen around us and the eyes turning our way. Then I slowly sit up and lean forward, placing my elbows on the table. Her eyes are glued to mine, unblinking as I tilt my head and try to figure out what she's talking about. Does she mean after I picked her up from the airport?

"Care to expand on that, sweets?"

She shakes her head so hard I worry she'll hurt her neck, meanwhile her hands are still clasped over her mouth. Then she jolts and grabs her bag and laptop, as though she's going to pack up and leave.

"Addison," I say, gentling my voice and moving to the seat next to her. "Wait, hang on a sec."

She pauses her frantic movements to look up at me again, and I try to offer a reassuring smile. I'm used to Everly's anxiety, so I use some of the things she finds helpful in the hopes it'll settle whatever is going on with Addison. I reach out slowly, giving her plenty of time to move if she doesn't want to be touched, then settle my hand on her forearm. I squeeze once and then nudge her hand away from her laptop.

She releases it and slouches in her seat, then glances around. Her shoulders hunch up and her cheeks turn even more red. I don't like her feeling self-conscious.

"Ignore them. A bunch of gossip-hungry vultures," I say, raising my voice enough for those around us to hear. There's a collective rasp of fabric against wood as people shift in their seats, pretending to go back to their own business. She takes a breath and meets my gaze again, so

I continue, lowering my voice for her ears only. "What did you mean? When did you want me to kiss you?"

Addison splutters. "I didn't—I mean, when we—"

I try not to grin, I really do, but it breaks through despite biting my lip to try to hide it. Her cheeks turn even more pink than they already were.

"Right, we can pretend you don't want me to kiss you, if that helps," I say. "And we can also pretend that I don't want to kiss you, either." I make a fist and bump it to my chest over my heart.

She looks shocked for all of two seconds before she grins and shakes her head.

"Fine," she says.

"Great, so you were saying?"

"After that drinking game when I was here a few months ago. I thought... I don't know."

"You thought there was something there. That we had chemistry," I say.

She neither confirms nor denies it, which I find slightly irritating because I want her to admit it. I want to hear that she felt—and feels—the same way I do.

"I thought we were flirting, and I guess I thought it might lead to more," she says instead. Her eyes are downcast again and I hate it.

"And you're wondering why it didn't."

"I'm wondering why you rejected me."

Oh.

That hurts. I hurt her, and that hurts me, and I don't want any of that.

"You thought I was rejecting you... No, no, sweet Addison." I shake my head and take a deep breath, trying to settle the emotions that are now roiling through me.

"I wasn't rejecting you, and everything you thought about us flirting, me wanting more, that's true. But we had both been drinking, and I didn't know exactly how much either of us had. I didn't want to take advantage, and I didn't want you to wake up the next morning with any regrets."

"I did, though," Addison whispers, then her sorrowful eyes rise from the table to meet mine. "I did have regrets."

My eyebrows draw in, the hurt spreading. Hurt for myself this time.

"You did?"

She nods, averting her eyes again. "I regretted not kissing you. I regret that I didn't put myself out there. I regret that I didn't make a move, and simply waited, hoping that you would."

This woman.

She might be the death of me.

"Addison," I whisper, and her eyes flick back to mine. "Can we start over?"

She blinks rapidly once, twice. A third time. Then a tiny, hopeful smile cracks through her vacant facade, and she nods.

"Yeah?" I say.

"Yeah," she whispers.

I stand, walk to the counter, grab a pink macaron, then stride back to her table. Her look of confusion transforms as I approach. She bites her lip, eyes flicking between mine and the macaron.

"Hi, I'm Frankie," I say, holding out the macaron. "I hear you owe the owner a few hours of cleaning, something about making up for a favor?"

Addison grins, all sparkling white teeth and pretty pink lips.

"I'm Addison," she says, "And I do believe you're correct. Shall I come back when you close?"

"See you at seven."

CHAPTER FIVE

Addison

I remember everything about you.

Frankie's words have been circling around my brain all afternoon. It shocked me when they murmured them under their breath, and I'm a little bit scared of the hopeful flame flickering to life in my chest.

It's a quarter to seven and I've been restless all afternoon and evening. I hardly ate a bite of dinner, my stomach too full of butterflies to have room for anything else. It's like the airport all over again.

I'm eager to go, to get back to Roasted even though I'm going to be cleaning, and I've been pacing for the last half hour as the time crawls by. I swear it started going backward at one point, but finally it's late enough that I can leave.

I hop on one foot as I attempt to clip my hair up and slide the strap of my sandal over my heel at the same time. All I accomplish is crashing into the closed front door, and I huff. Now my shoulder aches.

Moose gives me a pathetic look, like he can tell I'm a mess and feels bad for me.

"Oh you hush," I say.

He wags his tail.

As I take a slow breath, I slide the strap on my foot, then twist my hair into a knot and secure it with a large turquoise clip. The mirror by the door shows a harried face.

Not a good look.

I bite my lip and lean forward, as if that will somehow magically change my reflection, then pull a few hairs free, loosening the front for a bit of a windswept look. I'm hoping I can sweep Frankie right off their stupidly sexy combat-boot-clad feet.

While wiping down tables. Apparently.

I roll my eyes, but it doesn't stop the smile lighting my face at the thought of spending time with them and our silly deal. Deciding to drive into town instead of walk, I snag the keys and give Moose a smooch goodbye on my way out.

The drive flies by, because of course, after hours of impatient turmoil, now is when time decides to speed up.

When I park outside Roasted, I can see Frankie through the front windows. They're behind the counter, closing out the register from the looks of it. I take a moment to compose myself, hunching over in the front seat and shimmying my boobs in an attempt to get them to perk up a bit. They're not the biggest, only a handful each, but I have to work with what I've got.

The door chimes when I open it and step in, and Frankie's hazel eyes dart straight to me.

"Lock it behind, would you?" they say, and I nod, turning back to the door.

When I look back up, they're next to me pulling down the blinds, and suddenly we're in a space that feels much more private than I anticipated. I gaze around, taking in the cozy space. There are plants and knick-knacks interspersed with local art for sale covering the walls, a couple shelves of books, and a vintage grandfather clock ticking away. The mismatched wooden chairs are all pushed in, the table tops gleam with no crumb to be seen, and the scuffed wood floor is shiny, like it's just been mopped.

"You already cleaned," I say.

Frankie shrugs. "There's still some dishes in the back."

"I can do dishes!"

They lead me to the kitchen, turning the hot water on in the massive sink and waiting until it steams as it shoots out of the huge spray nozzle. The kitchen is minimal, no decoration and not much color. All industrial with stainless steel counters and cabinets, a shiny tile floor that's also been mopped recently, and a pile of dirty dishes. Clearly maximizing function and ease over anything else. I step up to the sink, glad I wore short sleeves as it's already warm back here, and pick up a metal mixing bowl and sponge.

Frankie stands next to me as I dunk, sponge, and rinse off each dish, then hand it to them to place into the dishwasher. Our fingers graze constantly, and I suspect they're doing it on purpose. I know I am.

I keep glancing to my right, eyeing Frankie from the corner of my eye. My mind is running faster than my heart can keep up with, despite how hard it's trying. I keep feeling their eyes on me too, and when our gazes collide, everything stops. I get lost in their hazel eyes, noting the sparks of gold and green flecked around the middle. Their lashes are dark and thick, indecently long, and from the looks of it they're wearing eyeliner but not mascara. I take in every detail I can, my hands working on autopilot as I barely pay attention to the washing.

"Oof."

The platter I attempted to pick up next is heavier than I expect, and it splashes into the sink when I lose my grip, bursting our moment.

"Well," Frankie says, wiping a streak of water from their cheek, then turning to look me over. Their lips quirk up. "I like your shirt."

I chose a pale yellow tee this time, with a hot pink, purple, and blue stegosaurus on it. Unfortunately, pale yellow plus water equals transparent, and my nude push-up bra is clearly visible behind the stegosaurus' plates.

"Of course," I say with a sigh.

Nothing to be done about it now. Thankfully I didn't wear something embarrassing underneath. When I glance up at Frankie though, they're clearly holding in a laugh.

"What?" I demand.

"I just didn't realize someone could make such a mess of washing dishes," they say, eyes flicking up and down my form. They reach up to swipe bubbles out of my hair.

"Oh hush," I say with a laugh. Then decide to lean into it.

I pick the platter up again, angling it as I lean away

from Frankie, and...

"Oops!"

It splashes back into the sink, this time shooting water in Frankie's direction.

"Hey!" they fling their arms up to block the water, but of course their hands and arms are already wet, and that just sends more water flying.

It breaks the ice, and next thing I know, we're laughing and passing dishes back and forth. I tell them about the antics Moose got up to this afternoon, and they fill me in on some of the town gossip. I'm a sucker for a reality show, and Stone Ridge could be up there with the best of them with the way this town's gossip mill runs. Everly never cares about what's going on around town, she hardly even deigns to mention Frankie, so hearing everything about everyone is a delight.

I learn that Alex, the local baker who makes all the treats for the coffee shop, has been experimenting with new recipes, but the older ladies in town hate it. They want the classics, so they've tried to boycott the bakery. Except there's nowhere else to get the baked goods they love so much, so they tried making them on their own, only to have the fire truck called to one of their houses when they started a small kitchen fire.

I can't stop laughing at how animated Frankie is. They wave their arms, use different voices for each person. They put their whole body into telling the stories, and soon we're not washing dishes anymore. Frankie is leaning against the counter across from me as we swap stories.

"Have you eaten?" Frankie says, pulling open the fridge. "I never ate the sandwich I made for lunch, you want to split it?"

They unwrap a sandwich bursting with veggies and offer me half, which I gladly accept. Frankie grabs a couple paper towels and angles their head for me to follow. I take in the serenity of the space as we make our way to the coffee shop couch by the front windows. Frankie sits down next to me, their knee bumping into mine when they fold one leg up. My appetite comes roaring back once my nerves settle, and I devour my half in only a few bites. I lean back against the worn cushions with a contented sigh.

Frankie dusts their hands off and crinkles up the wrapper, then angles their body toward mine.

"Thanks for coming over, I'm not sure I've ever had so much fun washing dishes," they say.

I grin in reply as my heart gallops in my chest, but I shrug one shoulder like it's no big deal. The movement draws their gaze down to my transparent shirt for a moment, though it's thankfully starting to dry now. More of my hair has come loose from the clip, and Frankie leans forward to tuck it behind my ear. It sends a shiver down my spine and their eyes heat.

"Can I take you out?" Frankie says, their voice strong, confident.

"Like, on a date?" I ask, wanting to be sure my hopeful heart isn't causing me to misinterpret and hear what I want to hear.

"Yeah," Frankie says, their crooked smile stretching to the side as they trace their fingers lightly down my neck, over my shoulder, and down my arm. "I'd like to take you on a date."

"Okay," I reply, immediately feeling embarrassed at how breathy that came out. I clear my throat and sit up straighter. "Yeah, I'd like that."

Frankie bites their bottom lip, catching my gaze. My skin heats when they release it and the color darkens, then their tongue swipes out, wetting it, and I've never wanted to taste anything so badly as I do their lips in this moment.

I lean forward slowly, closing the inches of space between us, my own lips parting as my gaze darts between their eyes and their mouth.

My phone buzzes across the coffee table in front of us, and I startle so badly I nearly leap out of my skin, banging my elbow against the arm rest. The buzzing is so loud in the quiet of the coffeehouse it sounds like some sort of alarm system ricocheting through the room. I press a hand to my chest, willing my heart to calm, and Frankie draws back with a resigned chuckle.

"You okay?" they ask, and I puff out my cheeks on a huff.

"Yeah," I say, tipping my head back.

The moment is broken, and when I check my phone, I have my sister to blame.

CHAPTER SIX

Frankie

I've never been so irritated with my best friend as I am in this moment. Did she have to call *now*? Addison jumps up and grabs her phone, shooting me an apologetic look as she does so. I swipe a hand through the curls on top of my head and take a breath as I overhear her reassuring Everly that everything is going fine and she has nothing to worry about.

"She was only checking in, guess she had a bad feeling or something," Addison says after hanging up. She walks back over to me, a small smile turning up her lips.

"So..." she says, and I love the look of mischief in her eyes. It sparks an answering desire in my own. "About that date."

"Yes?"

"I hear you've got a great view upstairs."

"You trying to get me to invite you up, sweets?"

Her cheeks pink and she bites her lip before answering. Her eyes are lit up, practically burning, and I know she's feeling the same way I am, but she slowly shakes her head.

"Not tonight, I don't think," she says.

I don't like the uncertainty that passes through her features. It speaks of past hurts, of wounds not yet closed, and I want to peel back her layers to see everything she isn't telling me. I don't have that right though. Not yet, so I nod.

"How about that date first," I say, biting back the words I want to let loose. Words like *what happened,* and *who hurt you,* and *how can I fix it?*

Addison nods, her features lightening again, and I tell myself to take it easy. There's something between us, and I don't want to mess it up by trampling her. I've already hurt her once; it won't do to be careless now.

"Tomorrow night? How about dinner? I'll cook. You can get that peek upstairs you were hoping for, no strings attached." I shoot her a playful grin, delighted to see a blush staining her cheeks.

I walk Addison out as we finalize our plans for tomorrow evening. She drove Everly's car here, but when she opens the door, she doesn't get in right away. Instead, she turns toward me and leans against the side of the car. I smile, knowing she's wondering about a kiss. I decide to do my best romancing, so for tonight, I lean forward and drop a barely there kiss, the softest I can manage, right on the corner of her mouth.

Addison's lips part and she sucks in a short breath, her blue eyes wide as she watches me lean back. I put my hand on the small of her back, urging her into the car.

"Goodnight, Addison," I say, closing the door behind her and stepping back.

It's the hardest thing I've ever had to do.

~~~

I stomp around the kitchen the next morning, practically throwing pots and pans at the sink as I remember the water turning Addison's shirt transparent last night. Jaime and Tori are both working today and they give me a wide berth, shooting questioning looks at each other behind my back. I know exactly why I'm grumpy, but that does nothing to ease the feeling.

I don't want to wait until tonight to see Addison.

I huff a frustrated breath, mostly annoyed with myself for how I'm feeling, and stride back through the door into the coffee shop. Then I halt in my tracks, blinking at what I'm sure is an apparition, but it doesn't go away.

There's an ethereal angel sitting in my coffee shop. An angel with glowing, light brown hair haloed by the sun
~~~

streaming through the windows. Sun that shines straight through her sheer pink shirt to the tight, burgundy-lace cropped top she's wearing underneath. A laptop open in front of her barely registers on my radar as her elegant fingers tap away.

The moment breaks when she glances up and her eyes meet mine. The smile that breaks over her face, I swear to all that is holy, causes singing to rain down from the heavens. Probably straight through that beam of sunlight highlighting her.

I blink, and she tilts her head, as though asking if everything's okay. I blink again, then force my lips to curve in response. It doesn't feel real, and suddenly I'm no longer frustrated or annoyed. Suddenly, everything feels right in the world.

I slip behind the counter to dump the handful of utensils I was planning to restock, and Tori's voice snaps me back into reality.

"You good, boss?" she says, and I nod.

My gaze slides back to Addison, her attention focused on her laptop again. God, this girl must be a witch. The hold she has on me after only a couple days. Did she slip me a love potion? I know I'm being ridiculous, but she's fried my brain. It's the only explanation.

I wander over to her table, trying not to show how desperate and eager I am for her company, her voice, her attention.

"You just couldn't stay away, huh?" I say, knowing I'm being hypocritical to the extreme.

Addison blushes, much to my consternation and delight, indicating that's exactly what's going on. She glares at me, or tries to, and I grin.

"Good," I say, folding my arms and leaning against her table. I angle my head down and lower my voice. "I haven't stopped thinking about you since you left last night."

She turns even more red, somehow, and I'm immensely satisfied with myself.

Her eyebrows raise, like she doesn't believe me, so I nod in emphasis as I straighten back up.

"Can I make you a latte?" I offer, and her mouth opens, but nothing comes out.

"Is that a yes?" I say, then chuckle. "Did you lose your voice? You haven't said one thing yet."

"Well, you haven't really given me the chance to, have you?" she says, all sass, and I'm obsessed. My eyes light up and she rolls hers.

"There it is. So, sweets, what'll it be?"

"Fine, you can make me a cinnamon latte."

"Oh, I *can,* can I?" I smirk, and she attempts to glare again, then lightly slaps my arm.

"You're a menace this morning," she says. "And I haven't even had my coffee yet."

"You're right, I apologize. I'll save all menacing until after you've had your caffeine fix."

"Thank you," she says, sticking her nose in the air, and I chuckle a bewildered laugh as I head back to the counter. I'm pretty sure there was nearly steam coming out of my ears only minutes ago, and now I feel like I could fart rainbows if I wanted to.

My gaze trips across everyone and everything else over the next couple hours, constantly being pulled back to the angel by the window. It just so happens that she can't seem to keep her eyes off me either, I note with satisfaction.

She starts to pack up sometime after the lunch rush, and I saunter over.

"Done for the day?" I ask, and Addison sighs.

"Yeah, I think I'm ready to call it quits."

"Hmm. Did you get any work done?" I ask.

Addison pauses her movements and turns to me, her eyes narrowed.

"What do you mean?"

"You claimed you were here to work, but it seemed to me that you spent more time staring at me than your laptop," I say, failing to hide my teasing smirk.

Addison turns that adorable glare on me again, and my smirk turns to a full grin.

"So what? Maybe I was looking at the menu behind you."

"So..." I lean in again, close enough that our noses are only inches apart. Her gaze flickers between my eyes and my mouth. "I liked it."

"Oh," she breathes, the word puffing against my lips.

I lean back, giving her space again, and she simply stares at me before ducking to hide her smile.

"Just to be clear," I say, "you *are* flirting with me, right? Because I'm flirting with you, but I can't quite tell..." I quirk a brow, and she blinks, then blushes, then breaks into a short laugh.

"Ugh, I thought I was so much smoother than this." Addison shakes her head as she speaks, a self-deprecating sort of crook to her mouth. "But you intimidate me, and I guess I'm out of practice."

"So, is that a yes? To the flirting?"

Addison lifts a shoulder. "I guess it's my attempt at it."

"Good, just wanted to be sure," I say, then I drop into the seat next to her and stretch out my legs, sliding one between hers under the table. She startles at the contact, then turns her wide eyes to me.

"Why do I intimidate you?"

"You, what?" Her voice is higher than usual, signaling her discomfort, but if we're going to move forward she can't be scared of me.

"You said I intimidate you, what about me makes you uncomfortable?"

"No, you don't make me uncomfortable," she says, and I pin her with a look, silently demanding the truth. "Okay, but not in a bad way. You're just, so..."

She waves a hand in a swirling motion in front of me.

"So *you*," she concludes.

"And that means..."

"That you're, you know. All confident and put together. You always know exactly what you want and who you are and how to do everything. You're successful, I mean, you own a freaking business." At this, she swipes both arms out to her sides as she gestures around us. I look around, taking in the space I practically eat, sleep, and breathe for. "Plus, you're Everly's best friend. Isn't that, I don't know, kind of forbidden?"

Well that was more than I was expecting. She certainly puts me on a pedestal, we'll have to remedy that at some point. If anyone belongs on a pedestal, it's her.

"Right, so you're intimidated because I own a tiny coffee shop in the middle of nowhere Arizona, I know how to pretend like I have my shit together, and Everly is my best friend. That about right?”

“Well.” She gapes at me. “That’s not really—”

“Addison. I’m just a person. Sure, I’ve known that I’m nonbinary since I was little, and when I see something I want, I go for it.” At this, I pause to give her another pointed look. She pinches her lips between her teeth. “I don’t know how to do everything, in fact I’d say I know how to do very few things, and of those, I only do a couple well. And Everly?”

I scoff, shaking my head. “She’ll be thrilled. Her best friend and her sister? I bet she’s going to screech about how happy she is that two of her favorite people are together. I’d put money on it.”

Addison blinks at me, dark lashes fanning over wide blue eyes.

“Us?” she says, her voice soft and hopeful. “Together?”

“I’d like there to be an us, and an us, *together*.”

I cross my fingers under the table for luck, even though I’ve never been superstitious for a single other moment in my life.

“I’d like there to be an us together, too,” she says. I reach across the table to free her bottom lip from her teeth with my thumb, and her beaming smile could light up the room.

“Good,” I say with a nod.

Her smile doesn’t abate as she turns back to her bag. Under her breath, Addison starts to hum along with the music playing in the background as she finishes packing up and stands. I rise with her, and to my surprise and delight, she leans over and places a sweet, soft kiss on my cheekbone.

“See you tonight,” she says, hips swaying as she saunters out my front door.

My grin is unstoppable.

CHAPTER SEVEN

Frankie

I'm walking through the front doors of the grocery store, mentally ticking off items I'd like to buy for tonight's dinner with Addison, when a body steps into my path. I scowl when I focus on the ruddy face of my least favorite person, Derek, the owner of our local grocer.

He steps into my space, far too close for comfort, and I try not to inhale the reek of cigarette on his breath and clothing. I take a step to the side, attempting to go around him.

"Excuse me," I say, trying to be polite.

Derek crosses his arms and steps in front of me again.

"I don't think so. You're not welcome here."

"Excuse me?" I say again, this time meeting his beady eyes with my own surprised stare.

"You heard me. I have the right to refuse service to anyone." He points to the sign on the sliding door behind me. "And I'm refusing service to you."

"This is the only grocery store in town," I say. I cannot believe the nerve of this guy.

He shrugs. "Not my problem."

I look around, not wanting to cause a scene, but there's literally nowhere else to buy groceries unless I want to drive an hour to the outskirts of Phoenix. I shake my head.

"Come on, man."

"*You* are not welcome here," he says, then takes a

menacing step closer and slowly raises his arm, pointing behind me at the doors. "Get out."

There's no one around to witness this incident, which is shocking considering it seems there's always someone gawking and waiting for the next piece of gossip. Myself included, though I can safely say this is not information I'll be sharing with anyone. I don't need or want the embarrassing attention it would bring.

I shake my head again and turn, deciding today is not the day to make a scene. I've had issues with Derek for over a year now. It started with him asking me where I source my specialty coffee beans, which I declined to tell him. I did a lot of work curating the perfect coffee blends, and I won't let an entitled man take advantage of that. He didn't like that I wouldn't tell him, of course, and I think that's what set him on this journey of destruction. He's one of those men who can't handle being told no, and when I didn't back down, it set him on the war path.

Since then, he's tried to get my business shut down for a number of reasons: not being open during during proper business hours, claiming poor customer service and discrimination, reporting Roasted for cleanliness concerns... all were dismissed because he's a blithering idiot just making shit up.

This is a new low, though. I wish he weren't so hellbent on making my life miserable, but I don't regret standing up for myself. If he continues to deny me entrance, I'll... Well, I'm not sure yet. Talk to the sheriff? Take it to the town council? I don't know, but for now, I need to figure out what I can scrounge up from my pantry.

I decide on spaghetti. It's nothing fancy, but I know Addison likes lasagna, and spaghetti isn't too far off that. I have some fresh herbs and mushrooms to add to the sauce, but when I go to prepare the garlic bread, I realize that not only do I have no fresh garlic, but I'm down to the dregs of my garlic powder.

"Great," I mutter.

I stomp into my shoes and run next door, figuring Mrs. Langdon, the crotchety old lady who owns the bookstore, has some I can borrow. I knock on her backdoor, hoping she can hear it, and soon enough she pulls aside a vomit green curtain to peer out the window. Seeing it's me, she scowls, then opens the door.

"Hi Mrs. Langdon," I say. "I'm so sorry to bother you, but I was wondering if you had any garlic I could borrow?"

"Garlic?" she says, narrowing her eyes at me and then darting her gaze in the direction of the grocery store. It's only a few blocks away, so her confusion makes sense.

I sigh. "Yeah, it's a long story. But if you have any, I'd appreciate it."

She harrumphs and gestures me inside as she shuffles down the hall. I step in and close the door behind me, then peek around at what I can see from the entry, hoping for a glimpse of her two cats. They're finicky little beasts, but one of them let Everly pet it once, and I'll never hear the end of it if I don't even up the score. No such luck though, and soon Mrs. Langdon returns with a container of garlic powder and a clove of fresh garlic, pressing both into my hands.

"That bastard still giving you trouble I take it?" she grumbles.

I freeze, my hands still outstretched.

"How did you know about that?" I ask, shocked, because I haven't said anything to anyone about Derek's behavior.

"I've got eyes," she says, her voice defensive, as though it should be obvious. "I know everything that goes on in this town."

"Right," I draw the word out, still not seeing how she knows so much when she spends her days shuffling between bookshelves.

"Well go on, then." She shoos me toward the door, effectively dismissing me. "Though I'm not sure garlic is the best choice if you want her to stick around..." she mutters under her breath, her voice trailing off as she wanders back down the hall, assuming I'll let myself out.

I gape at her back. *How* does she know about our date?

Then I look down at the garlic in my hands, wondering if she's right.

Addison

* * *

I text Frankie that I'm here and they throw the back door open, ushering me inside and up the stairs to their apartment loft on the second floor. They have a record playing soft jazz in the corner, and it smells divine up here. Like lasagna, actually, and my mouth waters.

"Dinner is almost ready," they say, then I catch a slight cringe as they continue. "Spaghetti and garlic bread."

"That sounds great!" I don't know what the cringe was about, but I love spaghetti and garlic bread.

"Make yourself at home," Frankie says, gesturing from the kitchen. "Bathroom is back there."

I wander into the living area, which is open to the kitchen, and start poking around. They have floating wooden shelves filled with books along one wall, and I grin when I see an entire shelf of spicy pirate romance novels, followed by another shelf of queer romantasy.

"See anything you like?" they ask, and I can hear the grin in their voice.

"How many can I borrow?" I say with a grin, pulling a pretty lavender book from the shelf to read the back.

They laugh, and I continue perusing, looking over the random knick-knacks, candles, and a few plants set in front of the corner window. They have a couple pillows on the couch that look out of place. They're fuzzy and look incredibly soft, but don't match the rest of Frankie's decor. I pick one up and fluff it before setting it back down.

"I got those for Everly," Frankie says, and I glance up in question. They seem to hesitate a moment, then shrug. "She likes them."

My brows pinch, as that seems a bit strange, to have special pillows for a friend who doesn't live with you, but then I realize, and nod in understanding.

"Her anxiety," I say, and Frankie nods, a look of relief on their face. They must not have known how much Everly has told me about her mental health. She mentioned to me when I was having a hard time that certain textures, especially blankets and pillows, help when she's feeling out of sorts. It's sweet that Frankie has them here for her. My heart swells with affection and gratitude.

We sit down to eat and I can't help the moan that slips

out when I take my first bite of pasta. It's delicious, with mushrooms and fresh basil in the sauce, and the perfect amount of garlic and cheese.

"Oh my god," I say around a mouthful of noodles. "I have no manners but this is so good, Frankie."

They grin. "I'm glad you like it."

I try to stop myself from eating too much, but I still end up feeling like a beached whale by the time we're done.

"I tried to hold back," I say with a groan as I sink into Frankie's couch. "Clearly it didn't work."

Frankie laughs and flops down next to me, angling their body so our knees touch.

My phone has been vibrating in my pocket all through dinner, and it goes off again now, only this time you can hear it rumble against the couch beneath me.

"Ugh," I say, leaning into Frankie so I can pull it out. I glance down, and all the tension I've been trying to leave behind floods back into me. My shoulders lock up and my jaw tenses.

I have notifications from both Sabrina and Benji. Multiple of them. So many that it doesn't even show me previews of all of them.

"What the," I mutter under my breath, my eyebrows drawing in with concern, a heavy dash of confusion muddling my thoughts.

"What's wrong?" Frankie asks. "Who is it?"

"My exes," I mumble, unlocking my phone to click through the messages. I check Sabrina's first, and they start out tame enough. The usual pleading for forgiveness, asking me to give her another chance, telling me she wants me back. As I scroll down, though, she starts sending pictures. Selfies of her wearing increasingly less clothing, a missed video call notification and her scolding me to pick up, a blurry image of her and Benji making out. And then the messages turn mean. Telling me I'm stuck up, a rich bitch, that I need to put out more and be open to exploring things if I expect anyone to give me a chance.

I can feel my face heating up, embarrassed and ashamed even though Frankie can't see the messages. There was a time when I thought she was it for me; when I thought we were perfect together. Turns out, I didn't really know her at all.

I click out of Sabrina's thread, not having read the last ones, and check Benji's. At first, his are similar to Sabrina's, with words of how much he misses me and wants me back, then trying to convince me to join a threesome with the two of them. When I scroll past a missed video notification from him too, with an all caps message to "PICK UP" followed by another missed call, his messages also turn mean. He calls me names, tells me I've never been worth it, that I'm a mess and a failure, that I'll never find someone better than either of them.

I don't realize my eyes are filling with tears until I blink and one runs down my cheek. Frankie, who had been giving me space, hears the tiny sniffle I try to hide, and when they whip around to face me, their face turns to a mask of horror. I don't blame them. Benji and Sabrina are right—I am a mess, and far more trouble than I'm worth. I've always been told I'm overly sensitive, and this is the perfect example.

Not wanting to face Frankie's rejection, or disgust, or disdain, I quickly stand and turn to leave. Before I so much as get a foot away from the couch, though, Frankie follows and their arms are around me. They pull me into their chest, arms circling my back, one cupping the back of my head to pull it down to their shoulder and the other squeezing tight.

I don't know the last time I was hugged like this. Maybe eight years ago, before my parents died? A sob hitches in my throat, and Frankie murmurs into my ear.

"It's okay, sweet girl, let it out."

So I do. I snot-cry into their shoulder, my chest caving in with the hurt that I've been pushing away and ignoring for months. I don't know how long it lasts, only that my tears eventually dry and my throat feels raw and I have a massive pile of tissues next to me on the couch that we must have sat back down on at some point. I pull back and wipe my eyes.

"Better?" Frankie asks.

I nod. "Thank you."

"What else can I do?"

"Maybe just some water or tea, and I'd like to wash my face, if that's okay."

"Of course."

Frankie shows me to the bathroom, snagging a washcloth from the linen closet and grabbing face wash from the shower, then promising to have tea ready before they step out and close the door behind them.

I take a deep, shaky breath, only belatedly realizing I left my phone on the coffee table. I'm glad I don't have it in here with me, though I do worry about what else they're sending. I take a few minutes to freshen up before wrapping all the tattered pieces of my courage around me and stepping back out into Frankie's apartment.

CHAPTER EIGHT

Frankie

I'm losing my mind, sitting here on the couch waiting for Addison to be done in the bathroom. My legs are bouncing, and my jaw is clenched so tight I fear I might crack a molar. Her phone keeps buzzing and lighting up with new notifications, and for some reason it never locked after she opened it, so I can see each text as they come in. Someone named Benji keeps calling her horrible names and telling her how unloveable she is, meanwhile a Sabrina is sending selfies, most of her making vulgar gestures.

I look up when I hear the bathroom door open, trying to soften my features. My heart is breaking for Addison, and I can't help but furiously wonder how long this has been happening. The hurt I glimpsed before, combined with the body-wracking sobs she let out when I was holding her, tell me it's been going on much longer than it should have.

Well, it shouldn't have been happening at all, but regardless, I'm determined to put a stop to it.

I want to open my arms, scoop her up and keep her safe next to me. I'm afraid of scaring her away, though. I can see how tremulous she is about this situation, her hesitance to stay here, and I know if I want her to open up to me I can't push too hard or fast.

So instead, I offer steaming decaf tea in a mug with a rainbow on it that says 'Sounds gay af. I'm in.'

She attempts a smile, but it doesn't stick, and I don't expect it to. As she sits next to me, her phone lights up again, and she startles with a look of panic when she realizes we can both see it.

"I saw some of them," I say, trying not to let the fury bleed into my voice. "I'm sorry for invading your privacy, but I'm not sorry I read them."

She doesn't reply. She also doesn't look at me.

"Can I turn it off for now?" I ask, and after a moment of hesitation, she nods weakly.

Thanking any holy beings that may be out there, I snatch the phone and power it down, then try not to smash it back onto the table.

"We don't have to talk about it if you don't want to, but also we can. Sometimes it helps to get it out."

Addison peeks at me from behind the rim of her mug as she takes a sip of tea. My eyes plead with her to confide in me, to let me help.

And to my eternal gratitude, she does. She cradles the warm mug between her palms as she spills the whole story, telling me about dating her coworker Benji, and how his actions changed the longer they were together, ultimately resulting in them splitting up. Her delicate fingertips trace the ridges of the rainbow on the mug as she continues, and she describes how she later met Sabrina and fell in love, only to catch her cheating with Benji a year and a half into their relationship.

Addison's voice wobbles when she gets to the part about breaking up with Sabrina last December, and it's everything I can do not to demand their addresses. I've always been a lover, but these two dickheads are really bringing out the fighter in me. My combat boots are ready to kick some ass.

I wrench my thoughts back when Addison pauses to wipe her eyes. I cup her face in my hands, angling it toward me as I brush away her tears with my thumbs.

"Every single thing they have to say about you is a lie. Don't listen to a word of it."

She averts her eyes, and I know she doesn't believe me. I'll prove it to her, though. It's just become my new life mission.

My fingers stroke through her silky hair as she burrows

into my shoulder. I suspect she's minimizing their harassment over the last few months, but I'll let it go for now.

"I'm sorry for ruining our date," Addison sniffles a few minutes later.

Her blue eyes are glassy and red-rimmed, her face washed free of makeup. She's so open and raw in this moment, I want nothing more than to kiss the life back into her.

"You haven't ruined anything," I say. "Thank you for sharing that with me."

She shrugs and looks away again.

"Hey," I say, and she glances up to meet my eyes. "I've got a gorgeous woman in my arms who's been letting me touch her and hold her all evening even though my breath probably smells terrible because, of all things, I made us *garlic bread* for our first date. If that isn't a miracle, I don't know what is."

That gets a small, genuine smile from her, the tiniest huff of a laugh, and we're back on the right track.

"I have an idea," I say, and I stand, tugging her up with me.

I grab my record player, then snag an album and jerk my head for her to follow me. Her deep sadness is turning into curiosity, and I know I've got her. She follows me up the narrow metal staircase to the roof, where I plug in the record player. I set my chosen album and turn it on, then crank up the volume. It scratches for a couple beats until the needle snags, and I sweep Addison into a dance.

I don't really know what I'm doing, but we're going to dance to Stevie Nicks under the stars and turn this night around. She giggles in surprise as I pull her against me, whirling us in a circle. I can bump and grind with the best of them, but I've never danced like this before.

Like it matters.

Addison leans against me, letting me lead us around the empty rooftop. A couple songs later, I break the easy quiet between us.

"When we were talking yesterday, you said me knowing what I wanted was intimidating."

Addison pulls back enough to look down at me as she nods, her eyes wary.

"Well," I say, "in this case, I know exactly what I want and I'm confident I know how to get it. I want you to be happy. Safe."

She blinks, her eyes glossy again, but no tears fall.

"And we're going to make that happen. Together. You aren't alone anymore, Addison."

A tremulous smile graces her perfect lips as she gazes through wet lashes like I've hung the moon. I haven't yet, but I sure as fuck will.

"Us, together," she whispers.

"That's right." I pull her close, so close there's not an inch of space between our bodies as our hips, chests, noses align. "You've got *my* intimidating ass on your side now, so anyone who messes with you had better watch out!" I say with gusto, spinning us around and squeezing her hard in emphasis. I'm being overly dramatic in an attempt to lighten what I know is a heavy topic.

Addison laughs, gripping me even tighter, and I pull her lips to mine for our first real kiss.

I pour everything I have into this kiss. My lips feel like they're on fire, my tongue impatient to taste, my teeth itching to bite and claim. I drag my tongue against her lips, tasting the salty remnants of her tears. She parts for me, opening so sweetly, and I sweep my tongue in, groaning at the taste of her. Somehow, the garlic is long gone. She must have put on chapstick or lip gloss, because she tastes like sweet berries and green tea with honey and something else that is all Addison.

Her arms circle my neck, her nimble fingers tangle in my curls. She's given me this one small piece of her, and I'm determined to have it all now. I want every piece Addison has. The hidden ones, the sad ones, the joyful excited ones, the hurt and broken ones. She's the most beautiful puzzle, and my most cherished treasure.

I grip her waist between my hands, then drag one up her side, barely brushing the curve of her breast. Addison whimpers against my tongue when I move past her breast to her jaw, angling her head so I can taste more of her. The moment stretches until we break apart with a gasp, both of us breathing heavy.

"That was," Addison trails off, her fingers brushing her lips as she gazes at me.

"Yeah," I say, still in awe that this stunning creature has chosen me.

Addison

We slow dance to a few more songs and I feel so cherished in Frankie's arms. They don't push for more, and while I burn for them, I also appreciate their restraint. Tonight isn't the night for it. Despite my impressive mental breakdown, Frankie seems to still want me. Snotty nose, puffy eyes, sweaty hair and all. It's astounding, and I'm having a hard time believing it.

Frankie insists on driving me home, eliciting a promise along the way that I won't turn my phone back on until tomorrow. They say we can do it together if I want, but I'm undecided on that.

"What if Everly needs something?" I ask as Frankie turns onto Poinsettia Lane, the road Everly lives on in our childhood home.

"She'll try you, and when you don't pick up, she'll call me." Their voice is so matter of fact, I have no doubt they're correct.

"Right, yeah," I say.

Frankie pulls right up to the porch and hops out before I have my seatbelt undone. They yank open the passenger door and drag me into their arms, folding me into a hug so comforting it brings tears to my eyes again.

"Thank you, Frankie," I whisper into their shoulder, unsure if it was loud enough for them to hear, but I'm too emotionally unsteady to say it again.

They squeeze me harder for a moment, waiting until my hold loosens to let go.

"You gonna be okay, sweets?" Frankie asks. Their strong hand is gentle as they sweep flyaway hairs away from my face.

"Yeah, I'll be okay."

"Will you come to the coffee house tomorrow?"

"Do you want me to?"

I'm letting my baggage get the best of me, but I don't have the strength in this moment to push back against it. Ever since my parents died when I was twenty and my sister and I lost touch for eight years, I've noticed the self-doubt and insecure thoughts gaining more of a foothold. Everly and I both withdrew into ourselves, hiding from each other and the grief associated with facing family. It was the loneliest time of my life, so when Benji started giving me the attention and affection I'd been denying myself... well. I stayed. Even when it turned into a super toxic—possibly abusive—relationship, and my confidence plummeted even more.

After that disaster, I finally found someone who treated me right that I thought was my person, only for Sabrina to cheat on me for months with my first toxic ex. It's safe to say my abandonment issues are thriving these days.

"I absolutely do," Frankie replies. "I always look for you, even though I know I can't expect you to get up before nine, let alone with the sun like I do."

I tuck my chin to hide the bashful grin upon realizing they already know I'm not a morning person.

"So yes," they continue, "please come to the coffee house tomorrow. I probably won't get any work done until you do, since I'll be glancing at the door every two seconds."

"And..." I look up, a spark of mischief entering my tone as my lips curve into a sly smile. "You *will* get work done once I get there?"

Frankie narrows their eyes playfully as their lips tilt into an answering smile.

"Cheeky little thing, aren't you?" they murmur, and my smile turns into a full grin, lighting a warmth in my chest behind my breastbone.

"I'm taller than you," I point out.

"Barely, and that doesn't mean you're not little," they say, backing me into my front door, then grasping the backs of my thighs and lifting me off my feet. My legs twist around their waist as my hands fly to their shoulders, but they're holding me steady. Frankie's hands grip my backside and their mouth finds my neck, sucking the soft skin between their lips.

"Oh," I gasp, rolling my hips into them for an endless moment until they release my neck with a soft nip, then a gentle kiss.

They pull back and lower me to the ground, looking at

the crook of my neck with satisfaction.

"There," they say, "proof. Now you have no reason to doubt me."

"Did you just give me a hickey?" I say, incredulous.

"Sure did." Their smug gaze flicks from my neck to meet my eyes.

"What is that supposed to prove?" I ask.

Frankie just shrugs and takes a step back. "Whatever you want it to prove."

They take another step back, tucking their hands in their pockets.

"Goodnight, Addison."

I'm left gaping as they turn and saunter back to the truck. I'm still staring when the driver door creaks closed and they raise an eyebrow, then nod their head behind me. They're waiting until I get inside, and I shake my head, a bemused smile twitching on my lips as I unlock the door. One last glimpse through the cracked door as I shut it shows a tattooed forearm propped on the steering wheel, hazel eyes glowing in the light from the porch, and a sultry, satisfied tilt of lips as they watch the door close securely behind me.

CHAPTER NINE

Addison

"I know exactly what we're going to do," Frankie says, practically jumping me as soon as I step into Roasted the next morning. Far too early in the morning, if you ask me.

"Um." I blink, taking in the bustle of the coffee shop and noting there's only one table open. Is this what the world is always like before nine a.m.?

"What?" I say, blinking again as Frankie bounces on their toes in front of me.

"Glitter bombs."

More blinking, some squinting, another glance around the coffee shop. Did they just say glitter bombs?

"What?" I say again.

Frankie's head tilts and they eye me. "Right, coffee first. Wait..."

Then they also glance around, their gaze landing on the vintage grandfather clock against one wall.

"Uh, Addison?"

"What?"

They grin and bite their lip, and I realize I've only said two words so far today, one of them repeated three times. I grimace.

"Did you get up early for me?" they say.

"No," I grumble as I try not to stomp to the open table. "You did!"

I can hear their grin as they follow me, and it tugs an answering smile from my lips. I absolutely did. It's impossible to be cranky around Frankie, even if it is an ungodly hour.

I slouch into the seat and set my yellow work bag on the table, then fold my arms on top of it and drop my head on them. Anything before nine a.m. is an obnoxious time to be awake. I hate it. My eyes are closed and I can feel the sun warming my hair through the window as I wonder where Frankie went.

My question is answered a few minutes later.

"Your coffee, my sleepy Addison."

Their Addison. I like that.

"Please," I groan, already reaching for the warm mug.

"Ohhh, I like the sound of that," Frankie winks and I roll my eyes. I'm not functional enough yet to deal with their flirtatious antics, but I like it regardless.

"I'll come back when you're awake," they say with a laugh and spin on their heel, black boots scuffing the floor as they make their way around the tables.

I sip my latte, confused by what flavor they added to it today. It's not one I've tasted before, and trying to figure it out helps my brain start to wake up. My eyes trail Frankie's curly head as it bobs and weaves around the coffee shop. I don't even pull out my laptop yet, knowing I won't get any work done and no one will expect me to be online this early anyway. Frankie's enthusiasm and charm fill the space, their laughter floating above the music, and I realize I feel at home here.

I'm not looking over my shoulder, waiting for someone I don't want to see to pop up and invade my space. I'm calm, content, and more carefree than I can ever remember feeling.

Frankie catches my eye and saunters over.

"You awake?" they say and I laugh.

"I'm awake," I reply. "Did you say something about glitter bombs earlier? Or..." Was that a dream? Did I imagine it?

"I did!" They plop into the seat next to me, snuggling their leg between mine under the table.

"Okay..."

"That's how we get back at your exes. We send them glitter bombs! They'll be living in glitter for weeks, months!" Their voice is so excited, I can't help but smile even though it makes me think about Sabrina and Benji again.

"Unless they like glitter?" Frankie says, dubious.

"I don't recall either of them having an inclination toward enjoying glitter."

"Excellent." Frankie claps their hands like a manic evil wizard.

"You're a bit devious," I say with a laugh. "I like it."

"Genius, right?" They grin, and I grin back, nodding my head. I think I like this plan.

Frankie asks for my phone, somehow already knowing I haven't turned it back on yet, and I dig it out of my bag. When I pass it to them, they angle it away from me, and raise an eyebrow in question before continuing.

I nod and turn away, looking out the window as I sip my coffee. I nearly moan at the taste, I have got to ask Frankie what they put in it this morning.

"Alright," Frankie says, an indeterminable amount of time later, as I spaced out a bit with my eyes closed and the warm sun bathing my face.

I turn back to them, not liking their serious expression.

"I think you should block them," Frankie says. "I also think..." but they trail off, not finishing the sentence.

"You think, what?" I'm apprehensive, assuming I'm not going to like what they have to say.

"I think you should keep proof of their shit, but I don't want you to have it. I propose that you let me take some screenshots, send them to myself, then delete all evidence so you never have to see it." Their words fly out rapid fire and it takes me a moment to catch up.

"Okay," I say. That's not so bad. I already told Frankie pretty much everything, and they saw enough when I was in the bathroom last night to know how bad it can get. I don't want to hide anymore, especially not from Frankie.

"Okay?"

"Yeah," I shrug.

"You're much more chill about this than I thought you would be," they say, almost suspicious.

"I'm sick of it. I've thought about blocking them before, but..." I don't want to say the next words. I already know how it'll sound and what Frankie's response will be, but they wait for me to finish. "It just seems mean, and I feel bad."

"Setting boundaries and protecting yourself isn't mean, Addison," Frankie says, laying their hand on my forearm. "What those two are doing is horrible, and by *you* allowing it you're also harming yourself. Blocking them, that's not mean. You're not doing anything wrong. They can still send whatever shit they want to, but they don't have a right to you. They don't get unsolicited access. There's nothing mean or wrong or bad about that."

"I know. You're right, and I know that, it's just hard to actually do it."

"Do you want me to do it?"

I consider for a moment, tempted to accept, but this feels significant and I want to do it myself. I shake my head.

"No, I want to, but I'd like you to do the other part first."

"The screenshots?"

"Yeah," I nod. "But, I don't want to see it. Maybe you could take my phone for a bit so I'm not as distracted by everything."

Frankie's hand squeezes where it still rests on my arm, then they tangle their fingers with mine. I look at their darker bronze skin, a soft contrast against my own sun-tanned coloring, and I like how we look together. I like their hand in mine, our fingers twisted together so there's no telling where one starts and the other stops. I squeeze back, then meet their steady gaze.

"I'll take care of it," Frankie says, standing with a chin jerk toward my coffee. "You focus on getting that beautiful brain online so you can get some work done and we can play later."

They smirk at the color I'm sure is tinting my cheeks. I don't know what "play later" means to them, but if it's anything like what it means to me... yes, please.

~~~

Frankie returns when they catch me leaning back in my chair a few hours later, arms stretched out to my sides. I got a decent amount of work done today, likely due to not having my phone.
~~~

"Get your work done?" Frankie asks. They lean one hip against the table next to me.

"For the most part. I'll have to head back so I have some privacy for phone calls, but that's it for today."

Frankie is holding my phone, tapping it lightly against their open palm, and I grimace when my eyes snag on it.

"Ready for this back?"

I take a breath and straighten my shoulders.

"I'm ready."

Frankie hands it over and pulls a chair out, scooting it right next to me.

"I think I want to say one final thing to them," I murmur, the thought only now crossing my mind. That I don't want them to have the last word. That I want to stand up for myself in a more direct way.

"Okay," Frankie says.

They slide a hand to my thigh under the table and squeeze once, their hazel eyes showing nothing but confidence in me.

I open my phone, seeing my message list devoid of both Sabrina and Benji. Frankie must have already deleted the message chains from both of them individually, as well as the group chat they added me to.

I start a new one with both Benji and Sabrina, and my fingers hover over the keyboard as I decide what I want to say.

Addison: You've both treated me
    horribly. I want you to know that this
    is it, I'm done. I'm blocking both of
    you and I hope you'll respect my
    request for you both to leave me
    alone.

I think about adding a "goodbye" or "thank you" — the polite, people pleasing side of me squirming with nerves at how direct and rude that message feels. But then Frankie nods slowly next to me. A slight, seemingly subconscious movement that I catch in my periphery. I don't think they intended for me to see it, but I do, and I hit send.

Quickly, I click into my contacts and find Benji first, hovering over his name for only a millisecond before I scroll to the bottom and hit the "block" button.

When I get to Sabrina's name, I hesitate. She was the center of my world for nearly two years, and the hurt I've endured as a result of her actions has been devastating. My heart is still bruised, confused.

Frankie tucks their chin on my shoulder, curls their arm around my waist, and their curly hair tickles my ear. A tiny smile tilts my lips at the sensation, at their nearness and unwavering support. It gives me the strength I need to block her too, and I toss my phone down with a puff of air.

Frankie kisses my cheek, then murmurs a quick "proud of you, sweets" before standing and returning to the counter and waiting line of customers.

~~~

The afternoon at Everly's passes slowly, and I keep finding myself checking my phone for messages in between calls, apprehension lining my gut until I remember that I blocked them. My two biggest mistakes won't be bothering me anymore.

I send Frankie a message, inviting them over when they're done with work, then I stare out the window, contemplating the position I'm in. I think I'm falling for them, but I'm also only here in Stone Ridge for a few more days. I don't know how we would make this work. I don't think either of us are cut out for long distance, and Frankie has only ever left this tiny town once. It seems like ages since they picked me up from the airport, but in reality it was only five days ago. Their entire life is here and I can't ask them to uproot everything for me.

And my life is in San Diego. My job, everything I know and am used to. The beach house I inherited when our parents passed that holds some of the most precious memories I have.

There's a tiny wiggle in the back of my brain, a thought gaining traction every time I avoid this topic. *Is it much of*
~~~

a life, though? I turn away from it again, not ready to face it yet, and focus on the excessively eager dog shoving a toy into my lap instead.

Frankie shows up later with a bag of baked sweet potato treats for Moose and his enthusiastic tail nearly takes out a side table. We spend the evening chatting, then making out on the couch like horny teenagers, then we get up and take Moose for a walk after dark when it's cooled off a bit outside. Frankie reluctantly gets ready to leave, and I begrudgingly let them, since they have to wake up at an unfathomable time for work tomorrow morning.

We spend too long kissing goodbye, yet somehow it's still not enough. Me pressing them up against the side of their beat-up truck. Their hands gripping my ass through my leggings. My hand cupping their jaw and tracing circles on the back of their neck. Shivers running up and down both of our spines.

Finally, we break apart.

"I really have to go," Frankie says. The stars twinkle in the night sky above us.

"I know,' I say, leaning in for more.

Frankie's lips smile against mine, then they nip my bottom lip and lightly push me back.

"Fine," I sigh. "I'll see you tomorrow, then."

Their truck rumbles down the driveway and I watch the glow of the tail lights as they turn down the road.

The last thought I have before bed is that I never did ask what was in that latte earlier.

CHAPTER TEN

Frankie

I get a weird vibe when I wake up, and it lingers as I do the morning baking and open up the shop. Like there's a cloud of apprehension following me around, or a ghost planning how to best haunt me.

I shake my head and send Addison a good morning text, though I know she won't be awake for another couple hours yet. I like to imagine her smiling first thing in the morning, and I hope to see it in person sometime.

I'm determined to make this work. Whether she gets that hybrid job or not, she's it for me. I don't know if she's realized it yet, but I'll do whatever I have to do to make it work.

Us, together.

I smile, and before I know it, she's walking through the door and setting up at her table. I contemplate my options for her latte today, deciding on salted caramel, and tossing a pinch of salt over my shoulder for good luck while I'm at it. More superstitious nonsense that I've never partaken in before, but the sketchy aura of this lingering spirit is *so* not my vibe.

I deliver Addison's drink and drop a kiss on top of her head, not wanting to bother her further as she's clearly in the zone this morning. She gives me a brief smile of thanks, fingers flying over her keyboard, then tips her lips up for a kiss. Her eyes never leave her screen, and I shake my head as I saunter away with a smile.

My hard little worker, kicking ass, taking names, and not putting up with any more shit.

Unfortunately, the same cannot be said of me.

I'm crouched behind the counter cleaning out the mini fridge during a lull when the door chimes and feet stomp up to the counter. I shuffle the various milk cartons back into place and am about to close the door when a booming voice sends my heart careening out of my chest.

"WHERE ARE THEY?" Derek bellows, and the coffee house goes silent.

I bang my head on the counter when I attempt to jump to my feet, and I already know it's going to leave a nasty bump. Tori is working the register and her terrified eyes flit between me and Derek. I motion her to the side and she scurries around me, shuffling away near the back exit.

"I assume you're looking for me? How can I help you?" I try to lock down my emotions, the confusing tangle of anger, fear, and exhaustion that this man won't leave me alone.

His face is red, his thick neck bulging over the collar of his wrinkled button-up shirt. He points a finger at me, his hand shaking with what I can only assume to be rage, though I have no idea what has made him so furious.

"You..." he says, leaning over the counter into my space. "You know exactly what you did!"

"I really don't," I say, holding my hands in front of me in a placating gesture and taking a small step back, thankful for the counter between us.

"I found your so-called supplier," he says, referencing the specialty coffee beans my shop is known for. I was never hiding it from him. All he ever had to do was sit down and research just like I did. Apparently, he finally got around to it.

"They declined to work with me, can you believe that?" His voice is getting louder, his face more red with every heaving breath and hate-filled word. "I know it was you. You put in a bad word about me, don't deny it!"

I didn't, but he wouldn't believe me, so I say nothing. It does sound like something he would do, though, so I'm not surprised he assumes others use the same shady business practices he does. I shake my head and focus on taking deep breaths through my nose to keep calm while hoping Tori has already called the sheriff. Clearly my supplier has good business and people sense; I wouldn't want to work with Derek either.

"You act all high and mighty, but you're a disgrace to our town. You don't care about other local businesses," he rages. "You're just a spoiled, selfish, disrespectful—" spittle flies across the counter as he speaks, but he's cut off from my view when a head of honey brown hair obscures it. A slender, lithe body steps between me and the counter, her extra inches blocking me completely.

"That is enough," Addison says, emphasizing each word, and I've never heard her sound so fierce. Her normally feminine voice is pitched low, so full of defiance and anger it makes my eyes flare and tingles shoot up and down my arms.

"I don't know you, but I know Frankie, and they are the least selfish person I've ever met." She reaches behind her with one hand and I grasp it in mine, tangling our fingers together. I attempt to step up next to her, but she shoves me back with surprising force.

"You talk about being disrespectful," she spits the last word, then pauses. I get the impression she just eyed him up and down, and I wish I could see the derision on her face that I hear in her voice.

"Yet you're the one barging into *their* business, yelling and throwing out unfounded accusations. Causing a scene, being a bully and frightening their staff." She scoffs with a gesture toward the back door where Tori disappeared. "You disgust me."

My heart skips a beat and my breath feels frozen in my chest. This is a side of Addison I could never have guessed at. I try again to step up next to her, but she whips halfway around, her hair smacking me in the face, to shoot a glare at me before turning to face him again.

Okay then, I guess I'll stay here.

"Well?" she demands, and I'm not sure what she's waiting for. She's already put him in his place.

"They're not a team player!" He sounds like a teenager throwing a temper tantrum now, and I have to hold in a snicker.

She lets out a derisive laugh. "Team player? For what team?!" she says, incredulous.

That's a good question, actually.

Derek splutters, and I imagine his face turning a delightful shade of burgundy with every second he can't come up with a rebuttal. Then the door opens and our local sheriff strides in.

"What's going on here folks?" he says.

Addison holds up her phone, the phone that is currently recording a video, presses the red stop button, then hands it to the sheriff.

"You can see and listen to it all right there. I think we'd all appreciate you removing this man before he causes any more harm to your local patrons," she says.

Addison finally lets me step out from behind her and I blink at her in surprise, seeing the sheriff doing the same before he puts a hand on Derek's arm to lead him away.

"You're a badass," I say, not even trying to hide the awe in my voice.

She smirks. "I learned from the best."

Her shoulders are rigid though, and I can see the clench in her jaw as she takes in the other patrons who are all still watching. Addison isn't confrontational. She couldn't even block her abusive ex without support, so the fact that she stood up for me like that in front of a room of people, to an aggressive man twice her size, has me wanting to kneel at her feet and worship her.

I would have handled it fine on my own. Certainly not as well as she did, but I would have figured it out. I didn't need her help, but she stepped in anyway. My sweet, bubbly, sometimes sassy Addison put herself in the most uncomfortable position she could have, for *me*. I'm desperate to sweep her into my arms. To kiss her until the tension drains from her body. To show her...

My thoughts sputter out.

I think I might love this woman.

~~~

The sheriff takes a report from each of us, and a few other patrons step up to offer witness statements as well. I'm so grateful for this supportive community. It's too bad Derek is a part of it, but I guess there are bound to be a few bad seeds.
~~~

I watch Addison as she finishes up with the sheriff. Her hands gesture as she speaks, her face animated. Scorn drips from her gaze every time she glances at the squad car where Derek waits.

I want to kiss her so badly. I wanted to kiss her that whole time. My lips tingle and I bite at them, knowing we're still drawing attention and not wanting to make Addison any more uncomfortable.

She finally walks toward me with a heavy sigh, her shoulders relaxing as she drops the weight she's been carrying. I glance at Tori behind the counter, raising my eyebrows to check if she's okay, and she nods. I pull Addison into the back room with me and sweep her into a hug.

Her arms tighten around me and her face nuzzles into my neck.

"Thank you for standing up for me," I say, rubbing soft circles on her back. "I know that wasn't easy for you."

"It *was* easy, though. I didn't even have to think about it," Addison says, pulling back to look me in the eye. "It was the easiest thing I've ever done."

A slow smile crosses my face as my eyes search her beautiful blues. They're brimming with sincerity and compassion, perhaps a hint of uncertainty.

"I wanted to kiss you senseless that entire time," I say, and her eyes flare.

She lets out a bark of laughter, then sees that I'm serious and her smile turns coy.

"Well," she glances around, "there's nothing stopping you now."

I grin. The cheek of this girl. I really, *really* like it. I cup her face between my palms and tug her lips down to mine, devouring her as I've been wanting to for the last hour.

Addison sticks around the coffee shop the rest of the day, and I offer to let her upstairs to use my apartment if she needs to make any phone calls. I get the sense she doesn't want to be alone, or perhaps she doesn't want to leave me, even though I'm fine. We both appreciate the connection and support right now, and I busy myself with work, though I can't stop the nagging feeling that there's something I'm missing.

That annoying sense of having forgotten something important lingers, but every time I try to focus on it, it disappears. Perhaps a specter has moved in and I didn't notice yet.

As soon as the last customer leaves, I quickly wipe everything down and practically sprint up the stairs. Addison went up with Moose about thirty minutes ago for a phone call and never came back down, and I'm eager to see her.

Ridiculous, considering I've been in her presence literally the entire day.

When I open the door, I see her sitting at my small wooden desk across the room with one of Everly's fuzzy pillows in her lap, and I smile at the ease with which she embodies my space. She's still on the phone, so I slip into the bathroom to quickly wash up and change.

When I come back out, she's done with her call and rummaging through my desk. I grin and shake my head. I don't mind if she's nosy, in fact I kind of like that she didn't ask before making herself at home.

But my smile drops when she says, "What's this?"

Addison holds up a stack of envelopes, and that thing I couldn't remember... it snaps into place in my brain.

CHAPTER ELEVEN

Addison

Frankie's smile drops and their face turns red with anger. I immediately backpedal, not expecting that reaction.

"I'm so sorry, I didn't think you'd mind," I blabber, the words flying out of my mouth with no input from my brain as Frankie crosses the space with a few quick steps. "I don't know what I was thinking, I didn't mean to invade your privacy—"

Frankie cuts me off with a kiss and I freeze.

"Shh, Addison," Frankie says, pulling back and swiping their hands over my hair. "I'm not mad at you, I like that you made yourself at home. I don't have anything to hide and you can snoop to your heart's content. I just realized something important."

"Oh," I say, my voice faint. This day has been the worst rollercoaster of all emotional rollercoasters.

They gently take the stack of envelopes from me, then turn to sit on the couch and lean forward. One by one, they take a folded paper out of each envelope and lay it open on the coffee table.

"Can you pull up that recording you took?" they say, gesturing for me to come sit next to them.

"Yeah," I say, clicking into the video as I walk toward the couch.

I hand my phone over, and Frankie pulls me down next to them, tugging me close so our thighs line up from knee to hip. Their leg pressing into me settles the anxiety that had started to swirl when I first saw their anger in response to the envelopes.

"What are these?" I ask, realizing each piece of paper has a typed letter on it, then looking at the envelopes sitting face up above them with no return address, no stamps, and no delivery address either.

"Frankie?" I say, my gut churning as I turn to them for an explanation.

They grimace with a sigh, then run a hand down their face before explaining.

"I've been getting these letters for a few months now," they say, gesturing to a handwritten date on the first one. March twelfth, just over three months ago. There's a second dated from April, then two from May, and another two so far this month.

"Okay..."

"The first couple were just angry messages, but then they started to get threatening. I'd find them slipped under my back door from the alley, no indication of who it's from and no way of seeing into the back alley since the street cameras don't record there." They pause and crack their knuckles, tension lining their tattooed forearm. "I thought about setting up my own camera out back, but I guess I didn't think it was a big deal. I don't know. Maybe I was in denial."

They pick up the first June letter, dated about three weeks ago.

"Something's been bothering me all day, and I think it was one of the things Derek said. It's the same as what this letter says."

They pass the note to me and I read it over.

> You act all high and mighty. But you're not tricking anyone with that nice act. We all know you're not a good person. You don't care about anyone but yourself. You're spoiled and selfish and this town hates you. You'll see.

I gasp, re-reading the lines that must have stuck out to both of us.

"It's been him, hasn't it?" I say. "Leaving these notes?"

Frankie nods, their expression weary. "I think so,

yeah."

They play the video, skipping through the first part to right before I stepped in front of them.

"You act all high and mighty, but you don't care about other local businesses. You're just a spoiled, selfish, disrespectful—"

Frankie pauses the recording and I suck in a breath, my eyes sliding between the phone and the letter.

"He messed up," Frankie says. "I always suspected it was him, I just never acknowledged it. I guess this is as close to proof as I'm going to get."

"You have to show these to the sheriff, Frankie," I say, my voice tight with worry. This borders on stalking, and would definitely qualify as harassment.

Frankie sends the video to their phone and nods in agreement, pulling up the non-emergency number for the sheriff's office. Frankie informs him that they have evidence they think incriminates Derek of further crimes. They explain, and also mention a grocery shopping incident in which Derek refused to let them into the store. I frown, not having known about that.

"Well?" I say when they hang up.

"He said to come by tomorrow, that he'd like to see the letters and try to get a fingerprint off them. Either way, he said it doesn't look good for Derek, and we can talk over some options tomorrow. I guess they're keeping him overnight at the very least, since I pressed charges."

"Good," I nod, satisfied for now.

Frankie gathers the letters and stacks them with their respective envelopes, touching them as little as possible now. The silence stretches between us, and every time they move, their leg rubs against mine.

Skin on skin, I can feel the heat of them, and my eyes drop to trace the line of their bare leg against mine. Their caramel-brown skin looks so soft, I ache to touch it. To trace the tattoo winding up their calf, to explore the hint of one I can see peeking out from the hem of their shorts.

My eyes trail up their body, taking in their muscular form and slight curves, until my gaze snags on their eyes. They're watching me, and my breath catches at the heat I see reflected back at me. Their hazel eyes look darker, here on the couch in their loft apartment, just the two of us in the quiet of evening.

A pulse of desire makes my heartbeat trip, and somehow I think they can sense it. Their eyes are burning, taking me in, observing every tiny response I make to them simply watching me. My eyes snag on their lips, their full, dark lips, slightly parted and slowly curling up on one side.

I know they're smirking, perhaps satisfied with the easiest seduction of their life. I don't care. I also know we're both full of tension, from the events of the last two days, but also from this attraction that's been growing between us.

I close the space between us, my eyes fluttering shut at the first sensation of their soft lips against mine. Frankie doesn't hesitate, either. As soon as I move, they meet me, with their hands gripping my hips and pulling my whole body closer, melding our chests and tangling our legs. My hands fly to their hair and I tangle my fingers in their loose curls, anchoring myself to them as our tongues dance and explore.

Frankie's mouth moves to the side, and they nudge my jaw up with their nose as they trail kisses down the curve of my neck. They lick behind my ear, then suck my earlobe into their mouth, and I ignore the whimper that slips from me at the sensation.

I feel them grin against my skin, and my hands grapple for purchase. I rake my fingers down their back, wishing I had skin under my palms instead of cotton, so I seek out the hem of their shirt and slip my hands beneath.

A huff of air escapes their lips, puffing against the curve of my collarbone when my fingers trace up their spine, pulling their shirt up as my hands explore. I want to see them, and I lean back, tugging on their shirt.

"Can I take this off?" I whisper, relishing their flushed cheeks. I'm sure mine look the same.

They nod, but don't wait for me to do it, grabbing the hem and yanking it off themselves.

I suck in a breath and another wave of desire pulses through me.

More tattoos. I trace them with my eyes, the one on

their sternum, mostly hidden by the binder they're wearing. The fine black lines along their collarbone beg for my tongue.

"You're so hot," is my idiotic response, and I flush with embarrassment.

Frankie grins, looking pleased at their ability to render me stupid, but it settles my nerves all the same.

They tug me behind them to their bedroom, and my eyes are glued to the delicate ink curving down their spine.

I think Frankie might kill me tonight. I feel faint already, and we haven't even started anything, not really.

Frankie spins around, taking in the needy, panting mess of a human that they've turned me into. They place a gentle hand on my chest and guide me to sit on the edge of their bed. Their fingers go to the hem of my shirt, barely grazing my skin, and I'm nodding before they can even ask.

Their hands are gentle but firm as they gather the material, slowly baring me to their hungry gaze as they pull it up my stomach, over my breasts and off. They hold my shirt in one hand, letting it dangle from their fingers as they take a half step back and bite their lip.

"Damn, Addison," they murmur, eyes tracing a path of fire across my skin.

It gives me the confidence to straighten, to push my breasts out and reach behind me to unclip my lacy bra. I let it drop, then lean back on my hands, putting myself on display as their breaths turn shallow.

"Your turn," I say, nodding to their binder.

Frankie doesn't hesitate, whipping it off and letting me look my fill. The sternum tattoo takes my breath away. It's an ornamental design, more fine lines that swirl up the middle of their chest and drip down toward their navel.

I reach forward, snagging a belt loop and tugging them into me. My knees part, allowing Frankie to stand between them as their mouth meets mine again. Our kiss is more frenzied this time, more needy as we both fumble with our shorts, sliding them off with hands from the other that aren't helpful but feel necessary anyway. I lay back and pull Frankie onto the bed with me.

Their hands roam, skimming up my ribs to cup my breasts and I arch into their touch, our mouths still melded together. They swallow my whimper, then pull back to look at me again, and their eyes snag on my hip bone.

"Addison," they say, low and husky, dragging my name out so it feels decadent on their tongue. Their eyes pop up to mine and I bite my cheek to hold in my smile. I knew they'd like that.

"What is this?" Frankie says, one finger tracing the tattoo peeking out from the lace of my panties.

"Why don't you find out?" I say. I'm momentarily astonished at my boldness, but it disappears when they grin and lean down, tugging at the lace with their teeth before their hands rip it down my legs.

Their fingers return to my hip bone, so lightly it raises goosebumps as they trace the small wave tattoo. My gaze turns from their fingers to their own underwear, and my hands reach to tug it down, but they strip it off for me.

"Tell me if you want to stop," they say, leaning over me again and kissing across my collarbone. Their mouth presses into the softness of my breasts, and I groan at their teasing as they avoid my nipple.

"Frankie," I say, grasping their hair and pulling.

They chuckle against my skin, then take my nipple in their mouth and suck, swirling their tongue around it before releasing it with a pop.

"Oh god," I mutter, my hips already aching to grind against them as they trail kisses down my stomach.

"Can I lick your pussy, Addison?" they say, and my entire body flushes at the dirty words coming from that sinful mouth.

I nod, but they wait.

"Yes!" I cry. "Please, yes."

And it's absolute bliss. Their tongue swipes up my center, splitting me open, and they suck on my lips before dipping in to taste me. I'm quickly lost in the pleasure, and I groan when they swipe my clit with their tongue and curl two fingers inside me, stroking that spot gently as well. The pressure is perfect, and my brain can't figure out which sensations to focus on.

"Where?" they ask, and it's something I've never been

asked before. My brain blanks, a lethal combination of surprise and desire.

"Tell me where," they say, their tongue slowly moving across my clit. When it hits the spot that makes my toes curl, I gasp.

"There," I say, my voice hoarse with pleasure. "Right there."

Frankie sucks my clit into their mouth and strokes that perfect, mind-numbing spot. I'm gasping, I can't get enough air, and my fingers scrabble along the blanket covering Frankie's bed. They grab my hand and move it to their head, not letting up on the pressure of their mouth, and then their free hand goes to my breast, tweaking and pinching my nipple.

My eyes roll and my back arches, my body caving to the pleasure as my legs tense on either side of Frankie's head. They hum, and it undoes me.

The orgasm crashes over me and I pulse against Frankie's tongue, around their fingers, my body never having felt anything so intense before as it lasts for moments, minutes, ages. My head is stuck in clouds of bliss as my body obeys Frankie's wishes, succumbing to their desires, submitting to the rule of their mouth.

CHAPTER TWELVE

Frankie

"Frankie, Frankie."

Addison gasps my name, coming down from the throes of her orgasm. I feel supremely satisfied as I lean back to take in her pleasure-wrecked body. Her soft brown hair spilling across my pillow, her long legs languid as they fall to the mattress on either side of me, her perfect breasts pink and heaving for breath.

I lean forward again to flatten my tongue against the tiny wave tattoo on her hip, licking it, then biting it, then dropping a soft kiss.

Addison giggles, goddamn *giggles,* and it's the best sound I've ever heard. Though her moans from moments ago are a close second. I grin as I pull my body up hers, dropping little nips and kisses along the way as she squirms and laughs beneath me.

I prop myself on one arm next to her, placing one final kiss on her swollen lips. I stroke the hair back from her face as she gazes up at me with those ridiculously blue eyes, still trying to catch her breath.

My own breathing feels unsteady in my lungs, like this moment might not be real. I can't fathom how hard and fast I've fallen for this woman, and to have her in my bed right now is a fantasy I wasn't confident would come to life.

Forget witches, are succubi real? I wonder. Those are the seductive demons, right? Addison *must* have some of that in her blood.

She interrupts my derailing thoughts when she angles up onto her elbow and pushes me flat to my back in the process. Her eyes are sparkling, her mouth tilted into a satisfied smile as she leans forward to suck the skin of my neck between her lips.

"My turn," she whispers, her lips moving against my throat as she licks and sucks, finding her own path down my body. Her fingers, then her tongue, trail along my collarbone and then down my chest. She pauses to suck first one nipple, then the other into her mouth, biting the buds lightly between her teeth and slowly increasing the pressure until I groan. Her eyes dart up to mine with a wicked smile, my nipple still trapped between her teeth and I throw my head back. I was right before, when I had the thought that she'll be the death of me. I don't know if I'm going to survive this.

I quickly realize she's tracing my tattoos as she brushes her fingers down my sternum and her lips follow the same path to my navel. But instead of stopping where I want her, where I need her, she skips past my hips and scoots her body down the bed, curling one hand around my ankle.

Her eyes meet mine again as she flicks her tongue out, connecting with the tattoo that starts on my inner ankle, right above the bone. My skin breaks out in goosebumps as she kisses and nips, licks and sucks her way up my calf, then along my inner thigh. She switches legs, going to the tattoo on my opposite thigh and following it up to my inner hip bone.

I angle my hips, desperate for her to touch me, and her breath ghosts over my lower lips. I unconsciously buck up into her and she huffs a laugh. A husky, sexy as fuck laugh that causes my core to clench around nothing.

"Addison," I practically growl her name and her eyes shoot up to mine. "Stop toying with me. Give me your mouth."

Her eyes widen and she clenches her legs together. My girl likes to be told what to do, and I'll be remembering that for later. She's hovering over me, not even an inch away from where I want her, her eyes locked on mine as she waits.

"Stick out your tongue," I say, and she does. No hesitation, her pupils blowing wide, she sticks out the prettiest pink tongue I've ever seen. I reach down with one hand, burying my fist in her hair to hold her steady where I want her, then I cant my hips and swipe her tongue across me.

I let out a filthy moan, then hear her match it and my pulse spikes. She attempts to lean forward, to put her tongue on me again, and whimpers when my unrelenting grip stings her scalp. Her eyes plead with me, and I hold her gaze for a moment, letting her know I'm in charge.

She blinks, and I loosen my grip, allowing her to lean forward for a second swipe, parting my lips and diving deep. She closes her eyes and an appreciative hum leaves her throat before her movements turn more frantic.

Realizing she likes this, that she's as desperate for it as I am, heats my blood and turns me on even more. I'm not going to last; I can already feel the heat building low in my spine, spreading to my core. I'm swollen beneath her talented tongue, and when she pushes two fingers inside me and curls them against my inner walls, my hips start grinding against her in earnest.

She moans and increases her pace, but that's not what I need.

"No," I instruct, "slower."

Addison slows back down, her eyes watching me attentively again. I like that she's lost in me, that she finds pleasure in giving me pleasure. I also like how submissive and responsive she is. Her tongue is perfect. Her fingers are divine. Her attention is heady, building my pleasure to heights I'm not sure I've felt before.

"That's a good girl," I say, hardly recognizing my own voice, and Addison groans. It vibrates against me, and that's enough to tip me over the edge. I tense and pulse, and Addison laps up everything I have to give, groaning again and extending my orgasm.

Addison's soft hands trace back up my tattoos as I come down to earth, sucking in air like I'm starved of it. She sends goosebumps zinging along my skin and I shiver, then yank her up into my arms. She laughs again, and I smile while planting my lips on hers.

I love you.

The words flit through my brain, but I manage to keep them in. It's too soon, right? It hasn't even been a week. I shake my head and turn my focus to the woman of my dreams, her body tucked into mine with our arms and legs tangled together.

She sighs, a happy, contented sound, and kisses my neck lightly. I kiss the crown of her head in response and we soak in the contentment for a few moments.

"You should stay," I say, my voice quiet in the silence of the apartment.

Addison looks up, her eyes searching mine.

"Yeah?" she says.

"Yeah," I nod.

A soft smile, hesitant at first, blooms across her face, but then it drops as her eyebrows draw together.

"What about Moose?"

I shrug. "I've got chicken we can cook him for dinner. He should be fine here."

Addison hums and tucks her head back into my shoulder.

"Okay, we'll have to remember to snag some of his food next time, though."

I grin, though she can't see it.

"There's going to be a next time, huh?" I say, my voice teasing as I move my hand from her hip to squeeze her ass.

And what a perfect, spankable, handful of an ass it is.

~~~

I wake to our bodies tangled together, with her face pressed into the side of my head, one arm flung over my waist and her legs fitted around mine. I have one arm wrapped underneath her, and I can't feel it. I hold in a grimace. That's going to be a bitch when I move it, but regardless, I don't want to. I want to hold her against me like this forever.

Unfortunately, the bliss doesn't last long, thanks to her wild hair. Her brown locks are lighter with the sun streaming in, burnishing her highlights to a gorgeous honey gold. That doesn't help the tickle in my nose, though, when a few stray hairs brush across my face with
~~~

each of our breaths.

I try to hold it in, clenching my chest and holding my breath, but it doesn't work. The sneeze bursts out of me, and Addison shoots up in bed.

"Holy shit!" she says, clutching a hand to her chest. I follow her up, reaching out to comfort her, when I sneeze again.

I fall back to the bed and roll my eyes.

"Are you sick?" Addison asks, her eyes tracing my face, looking for any signs that I might not be feeling well.

"Nope," I say, then tug a lock of her hair with a grin as I appreciate her naked form.

Her pretty cheeks flush and she pulls the sheet up to her chest. I angle myself up to lean into her, inhaling her sweet scent and pressing my lips to her throat.

"You're even more gorgeous in the daylight," I say, then kiss her lightly on the lips.

"Oh my god. Don't you have to work?" she says, eyes darting to the window as her voice rises with alarm.

"Nope," I say, stretching out on the bed and smirking when her eyes go to my chest. "I texted Jaime last night to open for me. Said I'd be in when I got in."

Addison looks at me with disbelief for a second before she laughs. We take our time getting ready for the day, sharing tender looks and soft touches before I head downstairs to check in and Addison leaves to take Moose home. Jaime has everything well in hand, although we're a little short on bakery items since I didn't get up to make anything.

At least we have Alex's usual delivery. The people will survive, I remind myself, then set to helping out.

When Tori arrives for her shift, I let them both know I'll be stepping out for a bit again, and they give me questioning looks. I rarely leave, and when I do, it's normally to go shopping for books next door with Everly.

This outing won't be nearly as fun, though. I have to meet with the sheriff to show him the letters and see what else can be done about the Derek situation. Part of me wishes Addison were here to go with me, but I know she has work to catch up on and this isn't her fight, despite what she might think.

When I walk into our small police station, it's early

afternoon already. The officer up front ushers me back to the sheriff's office without any questions, where I take a seat and share the information with him. I hand over the letters I've placed in a plastic bag, answering his questions and hoping I'm doing the right thing. I don't want to cause drama or disrupt the town, but in this case Derek brought it on himself.

I also play the video again, and he requests a copy of it to compare to the letters. He lets me take pictures of the letters before he puts them in an evidence bag to get tested for prints, saying it'll be a few days before they have anything concrete.

He does offer to help me file a restraining order though, which he suggested after I told him about Derek not allowing me in for groceries. I guess I have enough evidence, and considering Derek doesn't seem like the type of guy to let things go, I take the sheriff up on the offer.

I complete and file the paperwork, including a clause that would allow me to shop at Derek's store for one hour once a week with him either off the premises or confined to his office for that time (as suggested by the sheriff) and then I finally haul my weary ass out of there.

I'm sick of dealing with this, but I feel a heady sense of relief, too. A burden I didn't realize I was carrying is no longer weighing me down. I avoided dealing with Derek for so long, not wanting to cause trouble or start a local business war. Or even worse, make accusations and then not be believed. It feels good to have stood up for myself and done what's right. I know I need to make my own wellbeing more of a priority and this was a step in the right direction.

I see a missed call from Addison, so I call her back on my way out to my truck.

"Where are you?" she says. "I'm at Roasted but Tori said you left."

"Yeah, I went to drop the stuff at the sheriff's. Heading back now."

"Oh, right! How did it go?"

I fill her in as I drive back, and she proposes celebratory drinks. I don't feel like working, and Tori and Jaime have it well in hand, so I agree and we head down the street to the Sioria, Everly's hotel, which also houses the nicer of the two bars in town.

CHAPTER THIRTEEN

Addison

It's only mid-afternoon, too early for many others to be here on a random weekday, so we head into the bar and have our pick of the seats. I request something fruity and sweet, while Frankie orders a spiked Arnold Palmer.

"Not what I expected you'd get," I say, sipping from the straw that came with my frozen pink drink. It's sweet and tastes like summer. I suck down more of the alcoholic juice.

"What did you expect me to get?" Frankie says, one eyebrow cocked as they raise the glass to their lips. My eyes follow the movement and get hooked on their mouth as they swallow and then lick their lips.

"I don't know, something more badass I guess."

"You think I'm badass?"

I glance pointedly at their very badass boots, then let my eyes trail the tattoos lining their skin. They shrug and nudge their knee into mine.

"Oh wait!" I gasp, appalled. "We didn't toast or cheers or anything!"

Frankie holds their glass up, then says, "Cheers," when I clink mine to theirs.

"Oh my god, you're ridiculous," I laugh.

"Excuse you," Frankie says, a mock scowl on their face. "I'll have you know I'm very badass."

A laugh rips out of me as I tip my head back, loving this side of Frankie. I bring my glass to theirs again, relishing their pleased grin.

"I'll do it," I say. "Cheers to setting boundaries, standing up for ourselves, and not letting mean people get in the way of our happiness."

Frankie stares at me for a moment, then raises their glass.

"Yeah okay, I'll definitely drink to that."

They take a long gulp and the ice clinks against the side of the glass when they set it back down, half empty. We spend the next hour chatting, flirting, perhaps drinking a little more than we should on a weekday.

Somehow we end up on the topic of our current reads, and decide a trip to Crooked Books is in order. We wobble down the street, clinging to each other and laughing when I trip over the curb and stumble into Frankie's arms. There may not have actually been a curb there, but who's going to know? Certainly not us.

We stumble into Crooked Books and Frankie loudly shushes me.

"Shh gotta be quiet," they slur, "Mrs. Langdon hayfus— hates... fuss."

We take turns "shh"-ing each other as we weave our way to the back where the romance books are shelved. We're only a few feet from our destination when Mrs. Langdon pops out from the aisle next to us.

"Ah shit," Frankie says. "Shhhhoot."

"Shhhhh," I say, and Frankie stares at me.

"No shhh, she's already caught us," Frankie says.

I blink and look around, remembering we were being quiet to avoid Mrs. Langdon, not because we're in a library. Because this isn't a library. The harried bookstore owner is glowering at the two of us, her hands on her hips and a scowl lining her age-worn face.

"Oops, sorry," I whisper, and Frankie cackles.

Mrs. Langdon starts talking too fast for me to understand, something about hooligans and unnecessary noise, as she puts a hand on each of our shoulders and bodily turns us around. I don't know what she's talking about, we were being perfectly polite and neither of us was being loud.

She's muttering under her breath as she ushers us back toward the door, pulling us this way and that and scolding

Frankie. Apparently they 'know better' whatever that means.

"We jus' wanted a look, a book, Mrs. Langdon," I say, trying to plead our case. "Issssat too much to ask for?"

"In your current state it most certainly is!" she exclaims, opening the door and hustling us out.

I spin around, ready to ask for a second chance, but the door is already swinging closed. It snaps shut right in front of my nose and I pull up short, then see her flip the lock while glaring at me from just inside the glass. Her nose is only inches from mine.

I huff, then turn back to Frankie, only to see them folded over a few feet away.

"Frankie?" I ask, stumbling over to them.

They're wheezing, but when they look up, it's because they're laughing so hard they can't breathe. I don't know what's funny, but I start laughing too, and soon we're sitting on the sidewalk, leaning into each other with tears streaming down our faces.

When I can finally catch my breath, I ask, "What was so funny?"

"What?" Frankie says.

We both crack up again at that, and it's in this moment that I realize I'm beyond tipsy and well into drunk territory.

"I never," Frankie says between gasps of laughter. "I always wondered how... what it was like... to be kicked out by Mrs. Langdon!"

I stare, bewildered as they try to rein in their choking laughs.

Eventually, we help each other stand, then bob and sway our way back to Everly's house.

"Hi cute boy," I say, scratching Moose on his rump as his tail thwacks my legs. "At least you're happy to see us, yes you are."

Frankie orders pizza for a late dinner, and we settle onto the couch, flipping to a reality show on the TV.

It's not long before I'm tipping sideways, sinking into the couch and snuggling into Frankie as my eyes get heavier with each blink.

I feel arms around me, hear footfalls on the stairs, smell the comforting scent of the sheets on my bed. A wet nose presses to my hand before blankets are pulled on top of me and I curl into them with a hum of contentment, already sinking back into the darkness.

I hear a whine that almost rouses me, then a whisper as steps softly pad away.

"I know, I want to be in the bed with her too..." the voice says. A voice I really like, one that I wish would stay with me, but I'm not even sure if it's real, and before I know it, I'm lost to sleep.

~~~

I wake up the next morning to a slight headache, and the delicious smell of coffee with a side helping of embarrassment. Last night could have—should have—been a great night, but I had to go and fall asleep! Like some sort of amateur. My grand ideas of celebrating and then getting tossed around a bit seem unattainable now, after my abysmal performance last night.

I snag a throw blanket and wrap it around my shoulders, then take in a deliciously cozy looking Frankie sitting up on the couch. Sleep-rumpled curls, wearing only a button down flannel and sipping a cup of heaven. I walk right up to them, following my nose until it nearly bumps into Frankie's mug.

Frankie takes a sip, raising their eyebrows at me over the rim as my eyes follow the mug to their lips. After taking a sip, they barely tip it in my direction, and my hands dart up without my permission, slipping over top of Frankie's hands around the mug.

I inhale again, the comforting coffee scent easing the tension in my neck as I take a sip and close my eyes. I don't register the moan coming from the back of my throat, or that I'm still gripping Frankie's hands around the mug, until they pointedly clear their throat.

I open my eyes, only to realize I'm inches from Frankie, who didn't move back when I invaded their space. Our eyes catch and hold. Have I ever seen more captivating hazel eyes? Light brown with flecks of chocolate and gold, framed by dark, thick lashes. One eye has a tiny freckle right below the outer corner. I reach up with one fingertip and touch it, light as a feather, and then Moose shoves
~~~

between us.

The moment breaks as a slobbery toy is thrust into my thigh and I squeak with alarm as I attempt to hold my hands steady and avoid spilling coffee over all three of us.

"Moose!" I say, then slowly release my hands from the mug, although my eyes linger on the divine beverage a moment longer than necessary.

"I'll go make you some," Frankie says, humor lining their voice.

"Oh no, that's okay," I say. "I can do it."

Frankie just waves at me to sit down as they stride into the kitchen, returning a few minutes later with a basic vanilla latte.

"Thank you," I say, being mindful *not* to moan as I take a sip this time.

"No problem," Frankie says. "I gotta head out, though. I've left the kids alone at the shop long enough I think."

I nod, still lost in my coffee, and Frankie slips a hand through my tangled hair, then tilts my face up to theirs. They step closer and lean down, hovering over me on the couch.

"Will I see you there later?" Frankie says.

"Yeah," I say, my reply breathy as they lightly tug my hair.

"See you later, then."

A barely there brush of their lips against mine, and then they're gone, the truck rumbling down the driveway. I'm left with Moose giving me puppy-dog eyes and a disgusting toy that I pick up and toss across the room, smiling at his antics as he bounds after it.

Frankie

We spend two blissful days avoiding the topic of Addison's looming departure, "working" together at the coffee shop—Addison on her laptop and me behind the counter. Until I can't handle not touching her, which happens nearly every hour, and I wander over to rub her neck or twine my fingers through her hair or drop a kiss on her lips.

She smiles every time, sweet thing that she is, and it

lights me up inside. I know we need to talk about us. About our relationship, and what we're going to do when Everly and Asim get back tomorrow and Addison has to leave shortly after that. We both keep pushing it away to focus on other, more physical aspects of our relationship. That side of things could not be going better.

I suspect neither of us has a good answer to what we're going to do, though, and that worries me. I'm determined to make it work, I just need to hear her thoughts first. I need to hear her say she feels the same way, that she wants me.

That it's us, together.

Addison pops back into the shop right before closing this evening, looking like a sun-drenched goddess in the golden hour light and wearing a bright orange and yellow sundress. The hem hits a few inches above her knees, and the top ties across her breasts so there's a peek of skin just below them, two straps looping over her shoulders and down her back. I'm pretty sure she's not wearing a bra and it's turning my thoughts feral.

She saunters up to the counter, a sinful smile curving her lips. I lean over it, my hand automatically cradling her head as I pull her in for a kiss.

Tori walks out of the backroom and sounds like she swallowed her tongue.

"Gah, gross," she says. "Can you guys like, not do that right over the pastry case?"

I glance down, realizing she has a good point, then shuffle Addison down the counter until I can swing around the end and tug her body into mine.

"Okay for real? How about just, not in here at all," Tori drawls, and I cut away from Addison's lips again to glare at her.

"Go home, Tori."

"I haven't finished cleaning up yet."

"I'll do it," I say, needing to get her out of here so I can enjoy my woman.

"I can help," Addison chimes in, taking a step back from me.

I groan at the interruption but toss her a rag, then turn to wipe down the counter as quickly as I can. I glance up to see her bent over a table, short dress riding up her thighs as she presses onto her toes to reach all the way across. My breath catches in my throat and I throw my rag down, then slip up behind her.

I press my hips into her ass and Addison jerks up, a surprised "oh" on her lips.

"Don't stop on my account," I murmur, my hands gripping her hips as my breath ruffles the hair behind her ear. "You look good enough to eat, bent over the table like that. I wanna hike your skirt up and take a taste."

Addison's chest flushes and I grin. She hasn't moved a muscle.

"Maybe you need a cute little maid outfit. I'll put you to work and reward you for good behavior."

I feel her breath hitch this time and she turns toward me. I'm surprised she doesn't snark back at me, but when I see her biting her lip, blue eyes blazing with desire, an answering pulse heats my body. Is she into role play? Is my sweet Addison kinkier than anyone would expect?

"You like that idea, sweets?"

She nods, so I grip her hair in my fist and slowly lower her mouth to mine, taking my time devouring her until I'm satisfied that she's the perfect amount of boneless in my arms.

CHAPTER FOURTEEN

Frankie

I planned to make dinner for Addison again, having been officially allowed to re-enter the grocery store for my weekly hour of shopping, but I'm not surprised that she would derail those plans. I should have suspected she had her own plans when she showed up at my door without Moose.

She arches against me and I pull back, tugging her up to my apartment. We kick off our shoes and her hot pink toenails pop out at me. I hate hot pink. I tend to dislike most bright colors, and yet on Addison, they're perfect.

I sit on the couch, diverting her when she goes to sit next to me and tugging her down to straddle my lap instead. I tilt my face up as I lean back against the cushions, taking in the temptress above me. The succubus who seduced me with one glance.

The answer I didn't know I was looking for.

"What are you looking at?" Addison says, shifting her weight as her hands start to curl on my shoulders.

I slip one arm around her waist, pulling her against me, then drive my other hand into her gorgeous locks. I grip the back of her neck and urge her down, pulling her lips back to mine.

"You. Perfection," I murmur, right before our lips meet again.

I know she heard, and I'm glad, but I don't want to talk about it. Not yet. She's perfect in my eyes, and I'm greedy for all of her. I urge her to open for me and she does, allowing my tongue to sweep across her lips. I groan at the feel of her against me. Her weight in my lap, her breasts pressed to my chest, her thighs hugging me, her nails digging into my shoulders.

I slide my hand from her back to her hip, grinding her down into me, and she lets out a tiny "oh" of pleasure. I breathe that in too, taking everything and wanting more.

My other hand drops from her neck to her thigh, soft skin exposed where her dress is pushed up as she straddles me. The bright colors make her skin glow like she's luminescent. I palm the bare skin of her thigh, then drag my hand up her leg and under her dress until I meet the crease of her hip. I smile when I move my hand further, feeling a tiny stretch of silk.

She's wearing a thong, and when I run my finger between it and the skin of her hip, she arches into me, wanting more. I trace the soft material to the firm globe of her ass, kneading and squeezing it, and she grinds into me harder. My emotions rise and fall, a bewildering dichotomy clashing inside me. There's a sense of power in the way Addison reacts to my smallest touches, but also this insignificance in the face of someone so incredible. She's gorgeous inside and out, and it's beyond my wildest dreams to have this with her.

Every move I make, she meets it. I nearly combust when she angles her hips to allow my hand between us. I push aside her wet thong to find her slick beneath it. I'm going to have a wet spot on my shorts from her grinding on me, and it makes me want to purr with satisfaction.

I tease her clit, circling one finger gently, but she's having none of it. She presses down on me, then her demanding little mouth pleads, "More, Frankie." between gasping breaths and desperate kisses.

I angle my hand so she can grind her clit against the heel of my palm, and I curl two fingers inside her, letting her set the pace and pressure. She uses me for her pleasure, taking what she wants as she wants it, and I love every moment. I open my eyes as we kiss, wanting to see her body, her skin, the expressions that play across her face as she chases her orgasm. I can tell when she gets close, her inner walls fluttering around my fingers, and I speak against her lips.

"That's right, use me. Find your pleasure, dirty girl," I groan, kissing her between words. "Take what you want and drench my fingers. That's a good girl."

I whisper praise and filth into her mouth and she clenches around my fingers, biting down on a scream as she pulses around me. I rock her through it, kissing and sucking down her neck until she falls limp against me, sated.

Her heartbeat slows and her muscles relax as I hold her, winding down from her orgasm. She tilts her face up for a kiss and I meet her lips gently, putting all of my tender devotion into that one soft touch. I want this so badly it scares me. When I pull away, she opens her eyes. Eyes I never want to look away from. They're soft, and vulnerable, and hungry.

I can tell Addison wants her turn with me. I'm not ready, though, so we take a break for dinner together. My thoughts and feelings are a confusing swirl with her return to San Diego nearing. It's a shock to realize how much my heart is at risk. I don't know if I've ever felt this off-kilter before, or this unsure of my future and what it might hold.

I finally set my utensils down and lean my elbows on the table, my forearms folded over each other in front of me. Addison glances up and must see something in my face, because she nods and sets her utensils down too. She takes a quick gulp of water, then leans back and pulls one leg onto her chair, hugging her knee to her chest.

"We should talk," I say, and Addison cringes.

"Are you breaking up with me?" she says, eyes downcast.

I rear back. What the fuck?

"No!" I exclaim, and her startled eyes dart up to mine.

"No," I say, softer this time. I pull my chair around to sit next to her and take her soft hands in my work-roughened palms. I stroke my thumbs along the tan skin of her knuckles and her fingers twist to grip mine.

"What then?" she says.

"I really like you, Addison. I care about you so much. I've never been happier than I have been spending this last week with you. You're fierce and resilient, so strong and courageous in your vulnerability. I want to make this work, but…" I trail off, my gaze searching hers.

"But?"

"I need to know if you feel the same. I need to know if it's worth it to you."

If *I'm* worth it.

"Yes," Addison says. "Yes, you're worth it, Frankie."

Somehow she knew what I was saying, responding to my unspoken words. It makes my heart trip in my chest.

"You're everything. I've never met someone like you before…"

"Intimidating?" I say, attempting a joke, even though it cuts a bit.

"No, not intimidating." Addison's voice has turned soft, contemplative. "I admire you. You bring out parts of me I didn't know existed, and while those things I first said about you are true, you're so much more beneath the surface. You're more than a successful business owner, you're a staple of this community and so freaking resourceful it's incredible. You're kind and compassionate under that confident exterior, and you're the most thoughtful friend either Everly or I could dream of. You're loyal, dedicated. So yes. Yes, I feel the same. Yes, you're worth it. Yes, I want to make this work."

She punctuates each 'yes' statement with a kiss. One on each cheek, the last on my lips.

My eyes are glassy as I stare at this angel. Not a witch, not a succubus. I was right the very first time, a week ago when the morning sunlight cast a halo around her in my coffee shop. She's a heavenly gift, one that I certainly don't deserve, but that I will strive to every day.

Her eyes search mine, crystal blue and utterly enchanting.

"Us, together. Right?" she whispers.

"That's right." I stand and tug her up into my arms, banding them tight around her. She giggles and buries her face in my neck, then I take her hand and move us to the couch. She follows easily, so trusting.

I pull her legs over my lap and she tucks herself into my side, hugging my arm. We're sitting as close as we can —touching as much as we can.

"So, what are your thoughts, my sweet Addison?"

Her cheeks tint a lovely shade of pink, and I swipe my thumb over one tenderly. Then she puffs out a breath and slumps, her shoulders falling forward.

"I was hoping to hear back about that transfer by now," she says, confusion and concern passing over her features. "I think I *should* have heard back by now, so I'm going to plan for the worst and say it's not going to happen. So if we assume I won't be working a mostly virtual position, and that I instead have to continue in-person at this department..." she trails off.

"This is the department that Benji is in, too?" I ask. I don't want to bring him into our safe space, but I need to know what her concerns are, especially since they'll inform my own.

"Yeah. Honestly, I like my job, but if I don't get the transfer, I'll probably look for something else. I don't think I can keep working with him."

I squeeze her to me for a moment and she tips her head, laying her cheek on my hair.

"Plus, I don't know how we can be together if I don't."

"What if you do get the transfer?"

"Then we're set," she huffs a sad, wistful sort of laugh. "I'd only have to go into the office four days every two weeks. That would be easy to navigate, right? We could make that work. I could be here most of the time..." She pauses, pulling back to glance at me and I notice her back muscles have tensed beneath the arm I have slung around her.

"I'd love to have you here more. You can stay with me some nights, or if you're not ready for that, I know Everly would be happy to have you too. Or heck, stay at the Sioria! You know she'd give you a room free of charge."

Addison peeks up at me from beneath long lashes.

"You'd want me to stay with you? Like, multiple nights?" she asks, tentative and hopeful. My sweet, darling woman.

"Of course. I want as much of you as I can get," I say, squeezing her again in emphasis. "The real question is would you survive staying with me? I get up between four and five a.m. most days."

Addison's eyes bug out. "You're lying."

"I most certainly am not," I laugh. "I've been paying the

kids extra to open for me this week when I want to spend the morning with you, but that's not a long term option. Think you could handle it?"

"If by 'handle it' you mean curling myself into a burrito blanket the moment you leave me cold and alone in bed, then sleeping for another four to five hours, yeah. I suppose I could handle it." She's grumbling and pouting and it is *adorable.*

I kiss her nose and she scrunches it at me, trying not to smile. I love the thought of her curled up in my bed, cozy and soft with sleep, as I start work and open the coffee house downstairs. I imagine deciding what to bake based on what mood she might be in, the tantalizing scents of fresh muffins and coffee drifting up to pull her out of bed and to my side.

"Well, let's wait for a final verdict on the job. If it's a yes, perfect. If it's a no, we'll have to finesse our schedules a bit the next few weeks while you decide what you want to do," I say.

Worst case scenario, I'll pack up Roasted and move to San Diego. They're gay as fuck and would love a queer coffee joint, I'm sure I could make it work.

"Yeah?" she says.

Her eyes are bright with hope and I circle my arms around her, tugging her further onto my lap as I press my nose to her neck. I inhale the scent of her, allowing it to calm the worries still working their way through me, then I nod.

"I promise," I say, pressing my words into her skin.

CHAPTER FIFTEEN

Addison

Everly and Asim return the next day, pulling into the driveway mid-morning so I don't get a chance to go to Roasted as I normally would. Moose is ecstatic, losing his mind as he spins in circles and barks. Everly laughs at his enthusiastic greeting. Melodious and beautiful, it lights up her whole face as she bends down to pet him. Moose pounces on her, knocking her back into Asim's legs.

He scolds Moose, then scoops his hands under my sister's arms and easily sets her back on her feet. She tips her face up for a quick kiss before stepping past Moose and folding me into her arms.

I'm still not sure about our dynamic. I know we both played a part in the distance between us, until I showed up with no warning last December for the holiday party she hosts every year. I cringe internally. That wasn't my finest moment—making a spur of the moment decision to attend after breaking up with Sabrina simply because I didn't want to be alone for Christmas—but it seems to be working out okay now.

At least it's brought us back together.

"How was your trip?" I ask.

Everly squeals and holds up her left hand, where a new, glittering ring adorns her finger. A bright, colorless diamond, sparkling in the morning sun.

"OH MY GOD!" I shriek and launch myself at her, torn between snatching her hand and giving her another hug. I settle on some combination of both, one arm around her neck and the other grasping her hand for a closer look.

"ASIM!" I turn to him and my eyes feel like they're exploding from my head. "This is the most perfect ring I have ever seen in my entire life."

Everly throws her head back in laughter and Asim's eyes sparkle as his whole body seems to puff up in satisfaction. He remembers a few moments later that I had been speaking to him, and he gives himself a little shake as he tears his focus from his future wife and back to me.

"Thank you, I think she's quite pleased," he says, his accent drawing out the vowels.

"Pleased?" Everly scoffs, lightly slapping his chest. "I freaking love it and you know it, but if you've forgotten, I'm happy to remind you."

His eyes sparkle as hers dance with mischief and I don't want to know any more.

"Okay!" I say, clapping my hands. "You need help unpacking?"

I turn to the car, but Asim places a gentle hand on my shoulder.

"I've got it," he says. "You two go relax and catch up."

"Okay seriously," I hiss at Everly as we step inside and head toward the kitchen. I assume she's hungry after her travels. "How did you find that man?"

Everly laughs. "Oh, you know. An obnoxious poinsettia delivery combined with some light stalking, and bam. Perfect future husband."

She stares at the ring on her finger with hearts in her eyes and I roll mine. She's ridiculous but honestly, that summary was pretty accurate.

"Alright spill. How did he propose? I bet it was romantic. That man's gone for you."

She grins and shares the story. How baby sea turtles were involved, how she accidentally ruined his plans the first time, but it ended up being perfect anyway. She shows me pictures of their trip and my heart pangs at the joy radiating from the photos. I'm happy for her, for both of them, but also... I want that for myself.

"So..." she says, and the glint in her eye raises my defenses. "You and Frankie seemed to be spending a lot of time together this week…"

I blink at her. How does she possibly know that?

Everly must see my confusion because she continues before I get the chance to ask.

"Moose has a GPS tracker on his collar." She grins. A feline, satisfied, pushy older sister grin that I do not like the looks of.

Then I register what she said. My brain flits backward through the last week, and the full extent of what she's saying hits me. I spent hours at Roasted every day, with Moose. I also spent the night at Frankie's place, again with Moose. One glance at Everly tells me she already knows all of this. She's biting her lip and bouncing like she can't wait to hear what I have to say.

I sigh, "Okay, don't be mad—"

"What?" she squawks. "I'm not mad! Are you together? Please tell me you're together!" Her hands meet in front of her chest like she's praying and I slump with relief. I guess Frankie was right.

"We're…" I start, then stop. "I guess we haven't defined it."

I don't tell her what I was about to say. That we're *us*, *together*.

"Okay," Everly says, dragging out the word. "But?"

"But we're together, yeah, and we're figuring it out as we go."

Everly squeals and I jump as she leaps up from her bar stool to embrace me again. I don't think I've been hugged this much in years. I like it.

"I knew it! Gah, this is the best news ever! I bet you're stupid cute together. Oh my god, I have to call Frankie."

My face is turning more and more red with every word she says, and when Asim walks into the kitchen to drop a kiss on her head, he pauses.

"What's up?" he says.

I take the brief reprieve from Everly's attention to type out a quick SOS message to Frankie, informing them that Everly knows and is freaking—in a good way—but losing it nonetheless.

My attention returns to hear Everly gushing to Asim about me and Frankie being together and how cute and perfect we are. That sounds like a lot of pressure, and

Asim glances at me, probably seeing the beginnings of panic in my eyes.

"Ever," he says, swiping a thumb across her bottom lip. She seems to get lost in his eyes, going silent as he continues. "Perhaps give them some space to decide what they want. Hmm, love?"

She blinks, then nods, looking sheepish.

"Right," she says, turning back to me. "Sorry."

"All good." I let out a breath of relief.

"If you want to head over there, you can," she says a moment later, winking at me. I shake my head, resisting the urge to do exactly that.

"Nah, I'm not here for much longer and haven't gotten to see you at all yet. If you're not too tired, want to hang out for a bit?"

~~~

Frankie ends up coming over that evening after Roasted closes, swaggering into the house like they own the place.

"I brought tequila!" Frankie shouts, holding up a bottle of the dangerous liquid. The three of us groan, half exasperated and half apprehensive. The only time Frankie breaks out tequila is for drinking games, and Frankie is notoriously good at them, as I learned last December.

"What?" they say, sticking their bottom lip out in an exaggerated pout. I want to suck on it, and they smirk when they catch me eyeing them like I'm hungry. "I thought we could have a rematch! Another round of 'Never Have I Ever' so Asim can redeem himself."

"Hey!" Everly yells, scowling at her best friend as she places a comforting hand on Asim's chest. He's chuckling though, and my heart pangs at the ease between the three of them. They're clearly comfortable in each other's company, and I feel like the odd one out.

Frankie snags glasses from the kitchen, then plops down on the couch next to me. My cushion bounces and I start to tip into them, sending a stroke of deja vu through me. They tug me into their side and press a kiss to my temple. My eyes flit to Everly, only to see she's staring at us with a ravenous, eager expression, biting her lip to hold in a smile.
~~~

"I should have known you'd fall for the pretty, popular girl," Everly says to Frankie as they pour tequila into shot glasses, teasing both of us. "Everyone always did."

Frankie turns to me, a calculating look in their eye. I'm a couple years younger than Frankie and Everly, so we didn't see much of each other at school, only when Frankie would come over to the house.

"Hmm, she was, was she?" Frankie says, eyes drifting up and down my body. "Can't say I'm surprised."

I snag a glass and down the tequila, twisting my lips to the side as it burns my throat. Everly cackles, Frankie's grin turns devious, and Asim smiles, then murmurs something I don't catch into Everly's ear. She's a ball of energy bouncing on the couch until Asim pulls her into his lap and wraps his arms around her, dissipating some of her restless fidgeting.

"Enough chit-chat," Frankie says, clapping their hands then refilling the shot glass I drained. "Never have I ever, round two, begins now!"

We all groan, knowing Frankie is going to win as they always do, but ready to have a good time anyway.

The evening passes easily with all of us enjoying some good-natured ribbing until Everly and Asim head to bed early. Frankie and I can't get enough of each other. I'm desperate to spend every moment with them that I can, dreading the looming deadline ahead of me when I'll have to board a plane and fly away from them. I hate not knowing how long it might be until I see them again, not knowing what our future holds or exactly how we're going to make this work.

I check my phone constantly, hoping and dreading the email that never comes, informing me whether I got the transfer or not.

I spend the next two nights at Frankie's, both of us frantic with our affection, in denial of the short time we have left together. I eat lunch with Everly each day during her work break, and while I enjoy reconnecting with her, I'm fidgeting and restless the whole time. Itching to get back to Frankie.

I wake up early the morning of my last day here after spending the night in Frankie's bed, like my body wants to take advantage of every precious second we have left before I leave. Frankie is already up, as usual, but it's earlier than I've ever woken before. The sun is barely rising, streaking orange and pink across the brightening sky. It's too pretty for such a sad day.

I wrap a throw blanket around my shoulders, not bothering to change out of my sleep tank and shorts yet, then wander down the stairs to find Frankie in the kitchen. They're muttering under their breath, mixing batter like they're furious at it.

"Frankie?" I ask, my voice coming out raspy from sleep.

They glance up, shock flitting across their face at seeing me conscious this early.

"You're awake?"

"No," I grumble, shuffling toward them. "It's stupid early."

They grin and set down the bowl and spatula, wiping their hands on a towel before wrapping me up in their arms. I slouch and tuck my face into their neck, burying the tip of my nose in their skin.

"It *is* stupid early, how can I make it up to you?"

"Mmph," I groan, and Frankie chuckles. A quiet, wistful, slightly sad sort of chuckle. Or perhaps I'm projecting.

"How about a banana chocolate chip muffin?"

"Yeah, that."

I poke a hand out from the blanket and wave my fingers in a "give me" gesture, not yet moving my face from Frankie's neck, and earn another chuckle. My lips curve against their skin and I tuck my arm back into my blanket burrito. They squeeze me tighter for a moment before backing me into a counter, then lifting me up to sit on it. I scoot to get comfortable, then stick my hand out of the blanket again.

Frankie snags a muffin from the cooling tray, removes the wrapper, and places the still warm pastry in my hand. It smells delicious, and I let out an involuntary moan when I take a bite. Ripe banana and gooey chocolate flood my taste buds.

"Careful," Frankie warns when I groan again with the second bite. They've turned back to their baking and I pause, deciding if I want to push it or not.

I choose to enjoy my muffin, knowing that I can both

have my cake and eat it too. Or, in my case, have Frankie pretty much anytime I want, and also eat their delicious muffins. Semi-double innuendo intended.

Win-win.

I smirk at my clever early morning thoughts and take another bite of the muffin.

CHAPTER SIXTEEN

Frankie

I can't focus. It's Addison's final day here, and I've messed up the last three customer orders, misplaced a stack of cash for the register, and spilled an entire box of to-go cups. I've never done any of these things before.

It's because I don't know what's going to happen. I hate being out of control. I hate uncertainty, not knowing when the next time I'll see her is. I'm trying to plan for the worst while hoping for the best, but I'm not used to this. I'm not used to feeling so strongly for someone, or planning my life around anyone else, or even contemplating doing anything other than being here behind the counter of Roasted for the foreseeable future.

I throw my head back and sigh with aggravation when I realize I left the whole milk out of the fridge, and that it's been on the counter long enough to have left a large puddle of condensation around it.

Then I feel a gentle hand on my shoulder.

"Hey," Addison says. Her voice alone drains the tension out of me. "You okay?"

"Yeah. Just..." I stop and wave my hands around, dejected. "You know."

"Yeah," Addison says. "I know."

She tugs me into her slight frame and rests her temple on my head. I sling my arms around her waist and take a moment to breathe her in. Then I'm moving, pulling out of her arms and stomping over to Jaime.

"You good if I leave?" I ask, and Jaime shrugs.

"I guess. Will you be back to close?"

"Sure. Wipe down out here, I'll take care of the register and kitchen. Yeah?"

"Yeah, boss."

I'm already untying my apron and dropping it in a hamper by the back door. This broody bitch is taking the rest of the day off to be with their girl.

"Let's go," I say, grabbing Addison's hand and tugging her back to her table. I start packing up her belongings, and she laughs.

"Frankie, what are you doing?" she says, taking her laptop from me. "Slow down, what's happening?"

"I'm taking you on a date. Jaime's got it covered, let's go."

Addison is grinning, infectious in her joy, and I have no choice but to smile back. I wouldn't want it any other way.

She shoulders her bag and I grab her hand again, twining our fingers together as I weave through the tables to the front door. I nod at a couple of the locals hanging out, and old Nancy winks at me. She's a nosy bat, but I suppose I can't blame her for wanting a front row seat to the town's current hottest gossip. Which is Addison and me, unfortunately.

We stumble out onto the sidewalk and it's hot as heck out here. Naturally, I pick up the pace and she quickens her step as I pull her across the street to the ice cream shop.

She orders a bowl with one scoop. One *single* scoop, to my absolute horror.

"Oh no, absolutely not," I say when I hear it. "Two scoops minimum, with a waffle chip if you're not getting a cone. We're going all out today."

Addison balks and I raise an eyebrow, attempting to look stern.

I don't think I've ever had to be stern in my life.

"Fine," she says, crossing her arms as she turns back to the counter. "One scoop of strawberry, one pistachio, with a waffle chip or whatever."

"Hmph," I grumble. I'll have my way with her later.

"And for you?"

"Waffle cone please, three scoops. One espresso, one

candied pecan, and one brown sugar bourbon."

Addison's mouth has dropped open and I glance at her.

"Yes?" I say.

She snaps her mouth closed.

"That's just... such a weird order."

"Oh my sweet summer child," I reply. "This is the best combination you could ever ask for." I kiss the tips of my fingers and then spread them to the sky. "Incredible. Delicious. Ten out of ten, no notes."

"Okay," Addison laughs. "I'll take your word for it."

I pay and take my majestic cone while Addison accepts a bowl and spoon with her pathetic two scoops. I lick straight up the side, getting a taste of all three at once, then swirl my tongue over the top with a groan of delight.

Addison has stopped walking and is gaping at me again, her cheeks flushed. She looks so cute with her bright pink and green ice cream dripping off the spoon onto the concrete by her feet. I smirk. Poor thing, she's got no idea what she's in for today.

"You good?" I ask.

"Are *you*?" Addison shrieks. "That was..." She searches for a word before realizing she's dripping all over the sidewalk. She shoves the spoon in her mouth and swallows, then finishes her sentence. "Indecent."

I bellow a laugh. I suppose it was, and we're only just getting started.

We make our way in and out of each shop downtown, and I treat her to anything and everything I can. A trinket from the local handmade shop, a sugar cookie with rainbow sprinkles from Alex's bakery, a fruity candle that's layered pink, purple, and blue.

Finally we end up back at Roasted, right in time for me to finish closing before I pull her upstairs and into bed with me.

We make love slowly this time. With gentle fingers, soft lips, and tangled limbs. Addison moans as her body responds to mine. We lay next to each other and I suck on every part of her skin I can reach, leaving marks from behind her ear and down her throat to her perfect breasts, then across her stomach to her inner thighs. I want her to feel me for days. I wish she'd be able to feel me for weeks.

I circle my tongue around the wave tattoo on her hip

and become nearly feral with the thought of marking her permanently. I've never wished for a different job until this moment, but if I could tattoo myself onto her, I would.

I lick back up her body as my fingers tease between her thighs. She thrusts into me, burying my fingers inside her while she buries hers inside me too. We rock against each other, and our kisses turn desperate and messy as we lose our breath, our bodies tensing up as we both near the edge.

"Frankie," Addison moans my name and her free hand scrabbles for purchase.

I move her fingers to my hair, and the tight fist she makes sends tingles of sensation across my scalp. The pain turns to pleasure as she keeps moving against me, and we sink further into each other. My mind, my body, everything is pure bliss. Her very presence feels like ecstacy.

"Addison," I whisper, my lips moving against the soft skin of her neck. "My sweet Addison."

"Yes, Frankie. Yes," she says, both of our hips moving as we breathe each other's air and seek each other's pleasure.

"Oh," Addison pants.

I pull back just enough to see her, to watch her find her pleasure as her pussy clenches around my fingers. She grinds into my palm and the way she says my name, panting it like it's a prayer, a reverent, breathy chant, it's too much.

My insides clench as I watch her come apart, and my own orgasm crashes over me.

~~~

I'm sore and tired the next morning, my body wrung out and my emotions already drained, but last night was undeniably worth it. I attempt to wake Addison with a line of gentle kisses across her collarbone, but she swats at me and rolls over with a mumble. I chuckle as I memorize the sight of her in my bed.

It's eight in the morning, not that early for most folks, but Addison doesn't function before nine. If she wants to
~~~

make her flight, though, she needs to get up.

"Come on, sweets," I urge, rolling on top of her to drop a kiss to each eyelid. "Time to open these pretty blues."

"No thanks," Addison mumbles, tugging at the blanket in an attempt to cover her face. Too bad I won't take no for an answer this time.

"Five minutes," I say, then stride into my kitchen to start the coffee and pack us some leftover pastries for the road.

Unsurprisingly, she's not out of bed when I return. She's curled on her side, one arm hanging off the bed, and a tiny bit of drool leaking from the corner of her mouth onto the pillow. I grin and consider taking a photo, but don't want to embarrass her.

I wave the coffee below her nose, and her eyes flutter open at the same time her dangling hand reaches for the mug.

"Ah, ah!" I reprimand, pulling it out of reach. "Not until you've sat up."

Addison squints her eyes. I think she's trying to glare at me, and I pinch my lips between my teeth to hold in a laugh.

Regardless, she begrudgingly sits up, then proceeds to pull the blankets up around her shoulders. I should have thought of that.

"Nope, no blankets either."

"Ugh, Satan." Addison wrinkles her nose at me and this time I can't hold it in. Even grouchy Addison is too cute to get mad at. I belt out a laugh. My cheeks stretch around a smile that crinkles my eyes, but her cute little pouty lip holds strong.

"Yep, I'm an absolute demon. Here to torture you with waking up at a normal, respectable hour."

"Sure feels like torture," she mumbles, but her limbs are moving and soon enough her hot pink toenails are stark against my floor and I wonder if I'll ever see them there again.

She snags the mug and takes a sip, shoulders slouching as she nearly falls back into bed.

"Oh no you don't," I say.

I pull her up and tug her into the shower, turning on some music to help wake her up as we get ready. I let her wash in peace while I take care of a couple things. Hoping for the best, planning for the best, reminding myself that it might not turn out how I want it to... but better safe than sorry, right?

Thirty minutes later, I have a moderately caffeinated Addison bouncing into the front seat of my truck as I load her bags into the back. I eye the olive green one already there and wonder if she's noticed it.

Addison

I finally have enough caffeine in me to be present in the world, and I hop into Frankie's truck, buckling myself in without putting my coffee down. It's a classic hazelnut latte this time, extra sweet. Frankie must have assumed I'd need the extra dose of sugar for our early morning start. The truck jolts as they slam the tailgate shut and I turn in my seat, watching them stride to the driver's door and step up into the cab.

This last week has been like a dream and I'm dreading the part where I have to wake up. It's been too good to be true, and this feeling of apprehension, that something— everything—is going to go wrong in a moment, won't leave me alone. I turn the music up and distract myself by singing along as we rumble down the desert highway toward Phoenix.

Frankie glances at me every couple of minutes. Their eyes land on my thighs, bare skin beneath my frayed jean shorts, and my breasts, hardly visible beneath my baggy shirt, and my exposed collarbone and neck where I have my hair braided back. Sometimes they seem to scour my face, imprinting it into their retinas, so I do the same. Neither of us knows what tomorrow will bring, or the next day, or the next.

It's terrifying.

I finally pull my phone out, having been avoiding it all morning, to see a "have a safe trip" text from Asim as well as a novel of a message from Everly. I smile, though it feels a bit wistful.

My heart stalls in my chest when I check my email, and time freezes for an endless moment. My eyes feel like they're going to pop out of my head as they flick back and forth across the screen.

Then it clicks, and I let out an unholy screech as I fling my hands into the air. My phone goes flying, hitting the ceiling before crashing down to the floor, and Frankie whips around in their seat. The movement jerks their hand on the wheel, and the truck goes careening off the side of the road into the tumbleweeds and cacti. Frankie slams on the brakes, the back of the truck fishtailing through the sand as their eyes, wide with alarm, meet my horrified gaze.

CHAPTER SEVENTEEN

Addison

I shriek again as the truck swerves and dips, hitting a massive bump in the rocky sand of the desert and narrowly avoiding a saguaro before finally coming to a harsh stop. My body rocks forward and then slams against the backrest, the seatbelt tightening against me as one of Frankie's arms flings across my body in a valiant effort at keeping me safe.

"Are you okay?" they say, chest heaving for breath as they turn to me.

Their eyes search my body as their hands start patting every inch they can reach.

"Holy shit," I say, panting.

I hold a hand up in front of me and it trembles as adrenaline courses through my veins.

"Addison!" Frankie's hands bracket my face, turning my eyes to theirs as they search my head.

"Yeah!" I say. "Yeah, I'm fine. You? Are you okay?"

"I'm okay," Frankie says, running a hand over my hair to check for bumps as I realize with dawning horror and euphoria what just happened.

"Holy shit!" I yell, a manic grin spreading across my face.

"What?" Frankie says, panic lacing their voice. Their gaze searches me frantically, but they freeze when it lands on my smile. "Addison?"

"I got it!"

"Sorry?"

"I got the job! The email! Oh my god, I almost killed us, I'm so sorry," I say.

My emotions are going haywire, jumping from thrilled to horrified and back to ecstatic, then to doubt. My eyebrows pull in as I try to recall the email and can't picture it clearly. My memory of the last couple minutes is all fuzzy chaos.

"I mean, I think I got the job."

I start patting around, searching the seat and floor for my phone. Frankie calls it when I can't find it, and we hear it ring from deep under the seat. I bend over and snag it, then open my email again, my eyes searching for those magic words.

When I look up from my phone, biting my lip against the massive grin threatening to take over my entire face, Frankie is wearing a look I can only describe as cautiously hopeful.

"You..." They pause to clean their throat. "You really got it?"

I nod, my head bouncing so hard I can't see straight. Or maybe that's the tears starting to blur my vision.

"I got it," I whisper, then turn my phone so Frankie can see it.

They clasp one hand under mine, steadying my shaky hold as they read. I watch their face transform. As the doubt turns to confidence, the caution turns to eager anticipation, the hope turns to joy and pride.

"You got it," they say.

Rich, hazel eyes, glowing in the desert sun, look up from my phone and snag me in their depths. There's nowhere else I'd rather be.

Frankie drops the phone in my lap and yanks me in for a hug. "You fucking got it! I'm so proud of you."

"Thanks, Frankie," I say, wiping beneath my eyes before the tears can fall. I'll never have to see either of my horrible exes again. I don't have to even think their names if I don't want to; with this transfer, I shouldn't have to work or correspond with him ever again.

On top of that, Frankie and I can be together.

"Oh my god," I say, my breath coming faster again as those thoughts settle in. "Holy shit."

"Addison?"

"We can do it," I say, beaming at them, the tears in my eyes for a completely different reason now.

Frankie looks bewildered, and I almost feel bad for the roller coaster I'm putting them through.

"We can...?"

"Us, together," I say.

Before Frankie has a chance to react, I reach over and palm the side of their neck, pulling our bodies together and fusing our lips. Such soft, perfect lips that curve into a smile beneath mine.

"Hell yeah, we can," Frankie says, pulling away to tip our foreheads together. "Good thing I packed a bag."

"What?" Now it's my turn for bewilderment.

Frankie smirks.

"You didn't think I'd just let you go, did you? I haven't gotten my fill of you yet, sweets."

I blink at them. They packed a bag... they want to come with me?

Frankie jerks their chin at the bed of the truck and I twist in my seat to see an olive green duffle bag next to my luggage.

Frankie, still smirking, places one more kiss at the corner of my gaping mouth before putting the truck in drive and easing it back onto the highway.

~~~

I have no idea how they did it, but somehow Frankie got the seat next to mine on the plane. I don't think I look at my book once the entire flight, I just stare at them with a dopey smile on my face. I'm astounded that this person who has never cared to leave the tiny town of Stone Ridge before didn't think twice before hopping on a plane with me to another state.

"What?" Frankie says, glancing at me from the corner of their eye as we wait for our luggage at baggage claim.

"Nothing," I say, still grinning.

They smile back and sling an arm around my waist, tugging my body into theirs. They grab our bags one by one as they round the carousel and I order a ride.

My leg bounces with nerves during the drive, and my
~~~

smile has dropped into a nervous grimace.

"You okay?" Frankie asks.

"I'm good, just, I don't know. A little nervous for you to see my place, I guess."

"You know I've seen pictures and heard about it from Everly, right?"

"I mean yeah, but still. I've changed it a lot and it's..." I pause with a cringe. I was going to say that it's a lot compared to their place, which it is, but that seems rude.

"Bigger than my apartment?" Frankie says for me, one eyebrow raised.

I grimace and shrug. Of course they knew what I was going to say.

"Sweets, I know. I'm not uncomfortable with how much money you have, same as I don't care how much Everly has. I'm used to you rich folks," they say with a grin, bumping their knee to mine. "Besides, I'm doing just fine financially. If you want me to feel threatened, you'll have to try a lot harder than that."

"You sure it's not weird?"

"Positive."

"Okay," I say, slouching into the seat with relief.

"Although..." Frankie says, eyeing me up and down. "I never considered the idea before now, but if you want to be my sugar momma, I might consider it."

I gasp, my gaze flying to the driver who is clearly holding in a laugh as my cheeks flame. Frankie doesn't have much tact. They laugh freely and reach across the middle seat to take my hand, giving it a reassuring squeeze. Then Frankie rolls their window down, turning their face to the fresh air as it whips through their floppy curls. I trace the tattoos down their arm with my free hand, raising goosebumps along Frankie's arm as I go. They smile and close their eyes, head dropping back to the seat behind them.

~~~

"You're sure Everly is cool with keeping an eye on Roasted for that long?" I ask.

Frankie had called Everly from the truck as soon as they heard the good news, and she immediately agreed to
~~~

help out—for an entire week—while Frankie was gone. The two teenagers Frankie hired seemed to think Frankie was being silly for worrying that they couldn't handle it on their own, and Frankie rolled their eyes at their casual dismissal of the situation.

I know Frankie did a good job training them, though. They'll be fine, especially with Everly there if anything sticky comes up.

"Yeah," Frankie says. "It'll be fine, I trust your sister. She spends half her time at Roasted anyways. Stop worrying."

I'm unpacking my suitcase in my bedroom when Frankie wraps their arms around me from behind. True to their word, they didn't bat an eye at the multi-million dollar beach house I live in.

I turn in their embrace and twine my arms around their neck.

"Well, if you're sure you can stay that long," I say, "I've got an idea of something we could do..."

"Check out all your favorite local coffee shops so you can tell me how much better my mochas are?"

I laugh. "Sure, if that's what you want."

"Parade me around town and show me off to all your fancy, rich friends?"

"I don't have any fancy, rich friends, but I'll happily parade you around anywhere you'd like to go."

Frankie starts swaying our bodies slightly as they continue to tease me.

"You'll let me ravish you in every single room of this massive house?"

I grin. "Obviously."

"Am I getting close?"

"Hmm," I tip my head sideways. "Parade was kind of close."

Frankie's gaze darts to the side as their eyes narrow, trying to figure it out for real now.

"Give up?" I taunt.

"Fine," Frankie says. "What will we do?"

"Go to Pride, of course! San Diego is *so* extra. A month isn't enough for us, so we celebrate in July too. The parade is the day before we fly back, and there's always fun events, shows, music, drag, everything! The whole weekend! It's really fun, what do you think?" I end up talking so fast I wonder if they can keep up with what I'm saying.

Frankie is grinning, though.

"You know, I've never been to a real Pride celebration. Stone Ridge only puts up a few flags for the month and calls it good."

"I figured," I say. "Soooo is that a yes?"

"Yeah, sweets. Let's go to Pride."

Frankie twirls our bodies and dips me into a kiss. I laugh against their lips, then dance my tongue against theirs as they pull me upright and back us into the bed.

~~~

I go into the office for at least a few hours every day over the next week to get my old desk cleared out and pick up my new laptop, have IT get everything set up for me, complete all the transfer paperwork with HR, meet my new in-person coworkers and manager, and receive the key card I'll need to get into the new office building. We also do as much onboarding as we can while I'm in town, since I don't plan to be here next week.

When I'm not at the office, I'm working from home trying to close out my current position and ensure I have everything ready to transfer starting next week. I asked if it could be as quick a turn-around as possible, and HR didn't push back when I proposed a one week timeline.

On the one hand, I wanted to make the chances of seeing Benji as small as possible. On the other, part of me wanted to confront him. For the first time since we broke up years ago, I'm confident in who I am and my place in this world. I feel like I could hold my shoulders straight and look him in the eye without cowering or cringing away. I realize that knowing that, having the resolve and belief in myself, is enough.

In the end, I'm glad I didn't see him. He doesn't deserve any more of my time or energy.

Meanwhile, Frankie drives themselves crazy doing nothing while I'm gone, apart from texting me constantly. I've learned not to check my phone during meetings, since half the time they're sending suggestive pictures,
~~~

bordering on nudes. I try to tell them to relax, but I don't think they understand the meaning of the word. Their enthusiasm whenever I get home is infectious, their presence bordering on addictive. I already can't imagine my life without them in it.

When I'm working from home, Frankie does everything in their power to distract me, and I don't hate it. I swear they get sexier every time I come back from the office. Their curls get messier, their hazel eyes brighter, their forearms more stark, their tattoos more striking, their smile more dangerous. I end up working the oddest hours, because somehow I keep losing all my clothes in the middle of the day.

And I don't utter one peep of protest, because I wouldn't have it any other way.

"What if you were naked when I got home from work?" I say.

Frankie laughs. "Well, if it wasn't Friday, I'd do it. Kinda pissed I didn't think of that actually. Lucky for us though, you don't have to work tomorrow."

I kiss their bare shoulder.

"Lucky," I murmur, pressing a smile against their skin.

That's definitely true. I'm the luckiest woman alive.

CHAPTER EIGHTEEN

Frankie

Addison has more energy than should be legal for any single person to possess. Especially considering she's not a morning person, and it's seven a.m. If someone had told me she'd be up this early on a Saturday—and happy about it—I'd have laughed in their face, but here we are.

She's hopping on one foot as she attempts to tug a sock onto her foot with a toothbrush in her mouth and her hair already pulled back into a pair of neat french braids.

"Are you already ready?" she yells.

"Yes," I grumble, but it's a lie. It's all a lie. I'll never be ready for her, and I'm smiling, not the least bit annoyed at waiting on her. I'm constantly smiling around this woman, it's insane.

"No, you're not!"

Addison moves the toothbrush to the other side of her mouth as she bounces over to me, only one sock on. I raise an eyebrow and try not to laugh. She has no room to talk.

"You said you'd wear the sparkles," she says, toothbrush bobbing around her garbled words.

"Ah, that," I say, biting my cheek to hold in a smile. "I don't know how to put them on, figured maybe you'd want to help?"

I'm sure I could figure it out. How hard can it be to attach some sticky gems to my face? Addison beams though and her blue eyes light up. She starts to brush her teeth in earnest with one hand while grabbing my wrist with the other. I link our fingers together instead as she drags me to her vanity and pushes me down into the seat.

She disappears and I hear her spit into the sink, then she returns, fanning out a variety of designs in front of me.

"Which do you like?"

I try not to cringe. I'm not really the super colorful, rainbow, hippie type, and these are all more than I'd ever choose to wear myself. They'll look magical on her, though.

"Uhh, which are you wearing?"

Addison hums in thought, flipping through them before pulling out a design of pink, purple, and blue sparkles that will go under each eye, high on the outside of her cheekbones. She holds it up next to her face and grins.

"Yeah, this one for me."

"Alright, I'll have the same, but rainbow."

Somehow, her grin gets even wider.

"You want to match me?"

I snag her waist and pull her down into my lap.

"Of course I want to match you. Can't have anyone thinking I haven't snatched you up yet."

I kiss her nose and she giggles, then gets to work on our faces. Before I know it, I'm wearing more color than I ever have in my life and each time I blink, the gems on my cheeks twitch. It's annoying, but entirely worth the joy it brings Addison.

She pulls out her phone and turns on the camera, taking a selfie as she kisses my cheek, then hums a pop song about red wine as she saunters into her closet to finalize her outfit.

My jaw nearly hits the floor when she comes back out in a hot pink crop top, the bootiest of booty shorts, and white hightop converse with rainbow laces. She pulls open a packet of temporary tattoos in various rainbow and pride designs and wets a washcloth, applying them liberally to her arms and legs. She even puts one on the side of her neck. It's lips, rainbow lips, like she was kissed by a gay fairy.

I'm kinda jealous, but before I can think on it further,

she's tugging my arms this way and that, inspecting them.

'Ugh, you have no open spots! I'd have to cover some of your actual tattoos. Is that okay?"

I blink, forcing my gaze from her barely contained breasts that are within inches of my mouth, down to her hands, where I see she's still holding the tattoos.

"Sure, whatever you want."

Addison places a few of her colorful tattoos on my biceps, blowing on each to dry it and sending tingles across my skin every time. Then she coats those delicious lips in sparkling glitter lipgloss and I nearly die.

"Does this mean I can't kiss you?"

"On the contrary, please do," she says with a grin.

I take the invitation, and to my consternation her lips taste like strawberries. I groan, swiping my tongue across her bottom lip and into her mouth, then wrapping my hand around the bare skin of her waist as I tug her into me.

Addison pulls back with a laugh.

"I'll just have to bring this with me," she says, re-applying the lipgloss and then pocketing it. She tapes her ID and a credit card to her boob beneath the fabric of her top while I stare.

"Gotta be careful of pick pockets," she says. "You'll want to keep your phone and wallet in your front pocket. Also is it okay if I leave my phone here? I don't have anywhere to put it and we can use yours if needed, right?"

"Sure," I gulp, still staring at her, unable to believe this sparkling, colorful woman is my date. I'm going to be the envy of every person we come across, straight or not.

I grin. "Let's go."

~~~

Addison shows me her favorite spots in the local gay neighborhood, Hillcrest, where the Pride celebrations and events are located. It's all I can do to keep up with her. She bounces from one place to the next, easily navigating the crowds and saying hi to everyone she does and doesn't know. She somehow collects a string of rainbow Mardi Gras beads, which she winds around her wrist before tugging me to a bridge where we lean against the railing
~~~

and wait for the parade to go by.

She makes friends with the folks standing by us within minutes, and soon I'm pulled into a discussion of everyone's favorite drag queens. It's unlike anything I've experienced before and my heart is starting to feel too full. Like I'm *too* happy.

Is that a thing?

After we have flowers thrown at us, along with more beads, glitter, and confetti from the parade, we wander down the road toward where the block party will be held later. Addison drags me into a dessert shop where we share a bowl of gelato—three scoops—then she bops along the sidewalk as she jams out to the music blaring through the streets. It's incredible, seeing so many people of all walks of life coming together to celebrate each other and our culture. We make our way back toward where we parked a few hours later, and I notice a Pride flag flying high in the sky above us. It's massive, bigger than any I've seen before, and there are people of all shapes and sizes dancing together in the street underneath it.

I blink in wonder.

My heart is feeling too full again.

My thoughts snap back to the present when Addison's hand is tugged from mine, and I look down from the flag to see she's been swooped into a dance with a queen right there on the sidewalk. She's laughing, her head thrown back as the two of them shimmy and shake, twirling and grinding to the beat. I grin and pull my phone out, taking a video, then Addison asks her to sign her butt cheek where it sticks out from the bottom hem of her shorts.

The queen gladly does, of course, even putting on fresh lipstick and leaving a kiss next to it while calling her 'darling'.

Naturally, I can't let that go without meeting it, so saunter over to claim my woman. I tug Addison's sparkly lip gloss out of her pocket, coat my lips, and start planting kisses all over her bare skin. I bite her neck and press a kiss over the mark, wrenching a gasp from her lips. Then I reapply the gloss, and leave a sticky mark on her left boob. More gloss, bicep. More gloss, wrist, then next to her belly button. Addison's gasp has turned into joyful laughter and she twists her fingers into my hair, blue eyes widening when I yank one of her legs up, hooking it over my elbow as I kiss her inner thigh.

Someone wolf whistles behind us and I grin, leaving another kiss on the opposite knee, then the back of her calf. Finally, I turn her around, get my lips nice and sticky, and mark her other ass cheek.

I sit back on my heels, admiring my work as I squeeze her ass once, then move my hands to her hips and turn her around to face me again. Addison's face is flushed and her smile looks permanent when I stick the lipgloss back in her pocket and slowly stand, letting my fingers dance across her bare skin.

"Addison," I say, my voice husky.

"Yeah?"

"Move in with me?"

She grins, then bites her bottom lip.

"Yeah?" she says, voice tentative.

"That better not be a question, sweets."

I free her lip with my thumb, then wrap one braid around my fist.

"Let's try that again. Addison, my love, will you please move in with me?"

She shrieks, throws her arms around my neck and leaps into my arms. I catch her under her ass as she wraps her legs around me.

"Yes!" she says.

That's more like it. I spin her around, both of us laughing, then drop her back to her feet before bending her over backwards for another, harder kiss.

Someone whistles again, then there's cheering, whooping, clapping. I don't pay attention to it until we run out of air and I pull her back up to standing.

She's breathless as she looks down at me, her pretty blue eyes dreamy with desire. Then her gaze snags on my neck just as mine snags on hers. More color that wasn't there before.

Someone has thrown a rainbow lei over our heads, and when I look up, there's a circle of the gayest folks I've ever seen surrounding us. Cheering, clapping, sharing in our joy.

"Picture, babes!" someone yells, so I pull out my phone and hand it to them.

They snap a few shots and hand it back, then the crowd continues on their way. I click into the first picture when a notification pops up prompting me to accept an unknown airdrop.

I look up, my eyes darting around, to see the person who just took shots of us on my phone walking backwards away from me. They wink, smile, then spin around, disappearing into the crowd. I hit accept, and a flurry of pictures are sent to me. Pictures of me and Addison from moments ago.

I look back at my phone, angle it toward Addison so she can see, and we flip through the new pictures.

There's me kissing Addison's boob, her head thrown back in a laugh.

Me on my knees with her leg hooked over my arm, kissing her inner thigh with her hands tangled in my hair, the connection between our eyes nearly tangible.

Addison jumping into my arms, both of us laughing as I twirl her around.

Me dipping Addison into a kiss, her hands clenched in my shirt with one leg hiked to my hip, my arms bracing her with my hair flopping across our foreheads.

Addison standing back up, one hand cupping my face, her eyes full of adoration while mine are filled with love, the Pride flag waving in the breeze above us.

I lower the phone and look at her, seeing tears in her eyes to match mine. I stick my phone back in my pocket and yank her into me, holding her tight.

"Yes," she whispers.

I pull back, my body protesting even as my mind wants to see her clearly for this. I cup my hands around her face, swiping my thumbs gently across her sparkling cheekbones.

"I love you, Addison," I say, ignoring the tremble in my voice as I do my best to memorize this exact moment.

Addison blinks and a single tear falls, but she's smiling so hard I'm not worried for a second.

"I love you more, Frankie," she replies.

I can't stop smiling either. We stand there, grinning like fools and staring into each other's eyes until someone drunkenly stumbles into me.

I roll my eyes and Addison's smile turns wry.

I take her hand in mine, but that's not close enough for me. I wrap my arm around her waist, touching as much of her as I can, getting sticky glitter lip gloss all over our skin. I tug her as close to me as possible, and she tips her head down against mine. We wander the streets, stepping over colorful stray feathers and sparkling fake gems, never letting go of each other, our smiles never dropping. Simply sharing in the joy of those around us, together.

Author Acknowledgments

Writing Love You A Latte was a completely different experience than writing Poinsettia Lane. For one thing, I didn't want to write this story until I started it, and then I quickly fell in love with Addison's and Frankie's love story. I felt compelled to write it when so many people wanted more of Frankie after reading Poinsettia Lane. So on that note...

Thank YOU, my gorgeous reader. Thank you for reading my book(s), and if you have shared this book or told anyone about it, created content or recommended it on social media, left a rating or review, thank you so very much. It means more than I can express with words on a page at the end of a book. I hope you enjoyed Love You A Latte. For now, we're done with Stone Ridge, but I suspect we may return there at some point in the future.

AND BEFORE YOU TAKE TO SOCIALS TO YELL AT ME... sign up for my newsletter if you want to know what the mystery latte was that Frankie made for Addison. You'll love the bonus spice too, I promise.

There are a few people I'd like to specifically thank, without which Frankie and Addison's story would not have been written.

My dearest Alexandrantha, you are such a gem. Thank you for pushing me to start this novella, to finish this novella, to edit this novella, and to do all the other backend things for this book! (Let's all take a moment to say "Thank you, Alex!" It truly wouldn't be published without her). Alex, I appreciate you endlessly.

Thank you to my beta readers and authenticity/sensitivity readers: Allie, Cat, Sarah, Sophia, and Hannah. An additional note of appreciation for T. Thanks to all of you for your enthusiastic support on and off social media, and for your feedback helping to make this book the best it possibly can be!

Andrew. My love. Thanks for going on writing dates with me, for listening to my random rambles when I come up with ideas, for not getting upset when I wake us both up at 3am by dropping my phone on the floor while blinding myself in an attempt to write down thoughts that will be 100% incoherent in the morning. And also thank you for attempting to help me decipher said incoherent notes, perhaps someday we'll understand their meanings.

Lastly... one more thanks for the romance readers!

Wondering what the mystery latte flavor was? Sign up for my newsletter via the link on my website and get a bonus (spicy) chapter where you can find out!

Corina writes feel-good love stories with tension-building spice, funny and relatable characters, and Happily Ever After's that feel like a hug in book form. All of her novels are written in queer-normative worlds.

When she's not reading or writing, you can find Corina forcing snuggles on her dog, rollerblading with her husband, playing the piano, or embroidering everything she can get her hands on, including book covers.

Check out Corina's website for info on
upcoming romance novels:
www.authorcorinabair.com

Connect with her on socials:
@CorinaBairBooks on IG
Corina Bair, Author on FB